THE LONG FUSE

Alan White's novels have an authenticity born of personal experience. As leader of a commando unit in World War II, he made more than a dozen operational jumps into Occupied Europe. After the war he worked for the BBC in America. He then returned to England and wrote *The Long Day's Dying*, which enjoyed immediate success and was made into a prize-winning film. This was followed by *The Wheel* and *The Long Night's Walk*. He now lives in Ibiza. His other novels include *Climate of Revolt*, *Kibbutz* and *The Long Midnight*, which are all published by Pan Books.

By the same author in Pan Books

THE LONG MIDNIGHT

CLIMATE OF REVOLT

KIBBUTZ

THE LONG FUSE

ALAN WHITE

PAN BOOKS LTD

LONDON AND SYDNEY

First published 1973 by Barrie & Jenkins Ltd
This edition published 1975 by Pan Books Ltd,
Cavaye Place, London SW10 9PG

ISBN 0 330 24143 5

*Printed and bound in England by
Hazell Watson & Viney Ltd,
Aylesbury, Bucks*

Though in the trade of war I have slain men,
Yet do I hold it the very stuff o' conscience
To do no contrived murder; I lack iniquity
Sometimes to do me service.

Othello

PROLOGUE

January 1940

It had rained all day and the London pavements glistened, catching the light of the moon. Thin pencil rays stabbed from the fronts of the few vehicles that moved around Trafalgar Square, their beams illuminating little of the road ahead. The dark green Humber looked black as it turned right in front of the National Gallery, sped straight ahead down Whitehall, then turned left into a narrow alleyway between buildings. Half-way down the alleyway it stopped; the sergeant-driver got out and opened the back door. The general was still asleep.

'We've arrived, General,' the sergeant said.

The general stirred, woke instantly as old men do, and smiled at the sergeant. 'Here already, Warburton?' he asked. 'You must have made good time.'

The general rose from his seat and climbed somewhat stiffly from the back of the Humber. Sergeant Warburton handed him his cap, his stick, and a briefcase, then cast a valet's professional eye over the general's clothing. The general's empty sleeve was neatly pinned across his chest, but his top pocket was unfastened and his leather cigar-case was showing. Warburton excused himself, pushed the cigar-case into the pocket, and fastened the flap.

The general chuckled, but said nothing. Warburton had been with him a considerable time.

A sentry appeared out of the gloom surrounding the doorway. Sergeant Warburton stepped forward.

'Major-General Lord Finedon,' he told the sentry, who had brought his bayoneted rifle to the 'present arms' position when he saw the red tabs on the general's uniform.

Inside the house, Major-General Lord Finedon was greeted by a brigadier, a colonel, and a lieutenant.

'Would you care to come in here, General?' the colonel asked. The general turned right into a room at the far end

7

of the small hall. Inside the room an enormous wireless set occupied half of the wall space. A sergeant wearing the flashes of the Royal Corps of Signals was sitting at the wireless wearing headphones. When he saw the general he didn't rise, but sat 'to attention', a pencil poised over the message pad before him.

The back room was connected to the front door by a folding partition, panelled, as were the walls, in old oak. The partition had been opened. In the front portion of the room were several armchairs, a table, and a trolley carrying bottles and glasses. The lieutenant beckoned for the general to go into the front room, then hovered near the drinks trolley. The general sat down.

So far, no one had said anything other than a murmured greeting.

The general looked about him, relaxed and content to wait. The brigadier looked at the colonel, then at the lieutenant.

'Jolly nice to see you again, sir,' the brigadier said.

'You're looking fit, Tony,' the general said.

Then he turned to the colonel. 'How's that lad of yours, Willie? Nasty wound, that was.'

The colonel coughed, embarrassed. 'They had to take off his arm, Lord Finedon.'

'Ah yes, joined the club, has he, the one-armed warriors'. Still, it was his left as I remember. He'll still be good for tennis.'

He turned to the lieutenant. 'I'll have a pink gin, Freddie, and not too much pink, eh?'

The general looked at each of them as Freddie made his drink.

'What's it all about, eh?' he asked finally, since he realized not one of them could open the conversation. 'What is it you do here, eh? Something with wireless?' He got to his feet and walked back into the next room, looked over the wireless operator's shoulder. The sergeant stiffened.

'Relax, man, I'm not going to eat you,' the general said. Then he reached over the operator's shoulder and expertly turned the switch that connected the loud-speaker and disconnected the headphones. The sound of music boomed suddenly through the room, a German cabaret song. The general hummed the music, and sang the words in company with the performer, *'Jede Frau hat irgen deine Sehnsucht...'*

'Lovely song, eh?' he said. 'You can't beat the Germans for cabaret. What station are you listening to? Berlin?'

The wireless operator had released his headphones from his ears. 'Yes, sir. Berlin, sir.'

The general went back and sat in the chair, accepting the pink gin Freddie offered. 'Right-o, Tony,' he said. 'What's it all about? Did you bring me here just to listen to the wireless?'

'Yes, sir, I'm afraid we did.'

'Afraid ... ? It's a long way to come, from Atherton. Just to listen to a wireless. I hope you've found a good programme for me ...'

The brigadier looked at his watch. The general was sipping his drink. The brigadier nodded to the other officers who quickly left the room. Ten seconds to ten o'clock. The song came to an end, and there was a short pause before the station announcer blandly said, *'Hier ist der Deutsche Rundfunk aus Berlin.'* Another silence; then a female voice. *'Guten Abend, liebe Hoerer und Hoererinnen,'* the voice said. It was warm and rich, easy and skilled. *'Und jetzt, "Stimme aus Berlin". Es spricht David Hinton.'*

Slowly, somewhat hesitantly, the voice of David Hinton began. It was a voice both men in that room knew well.

'There was a time,' David Hinton said, his German articulation very precise, *'when I was proud to have been born of a long line of Englishmen ...'*

A burst of aerial static obliterated the next few words; the brigadier looked at the wireless operator who turned a dial, trimming out the interference. When the voice returned, it was loud, clear, and quite unmistakable.

'Let me now tell you,' the voice said, *'when and why I became ashamed of being English ...'*

'That's David,' the general said, uncomprehending. He

9

looked at the brigadier. 'That's David. What the hell's my boy doing, broadcasting for the Nazis?'

But then the truth hammered him; his face rapidly turned the colour of old pewter, and he slumped unconscious in his chair. The brigadier got to the chair in a fraction of a second and held the general's head, placing his other hand inside the general's tunic, feeling for a heart-beat.

The voice of David Hinton, the general's son, filled the room, broadcasting from Berlin. *'There is a growing feeling in England,'* David Hinton said, *'that this war is being fought for the benefit of a privileged few ...'*

'Turn that bloody thing off, Sergeant,' the brigadier said.

CHAPTER ONE

David Hinton was born in 1915, the second son of Lord Finedon. His mother had been a keen horsewoman until the birth of David, premature and by caesarian section, ended her hopes of a place in the Olympic team. She became a semi-invalid; the baby saw her only by appointment and for short periods of time, being left in the care first of a nurse and later of a governess, in the family seat in Northamptonshire.

As soon as he was old enough, David was sent to Eton; holidays were spent on the Continent with a specially engaged tutor. By the time he went up to Magdalen, Oxford, he was already tri-lingual in English, French and German with an extensive knowledge of the literature of those countries. He took a First in 1937, and was immediately offered junior rank in the Foreign Service.

In 1937 David Hinton was posted to the British Embassy in Berlin as a junior officer in the cultural section; routine reports on him and his work described a donnish young man. He quickly grasped the essentials of the German *Kultur* in those pre-war days, and often was asked to advise the political section.

When the Embassy closed in 1939 and its staff dispersed, David Hinton disappeared. He was not heard of for the first two months of the war and nothing was known of his activities until his father, Major-General Lord Finedon, summoned to the War Office one evening, verified the identification of a voice broadcasting over the German National Radio Service as that of his son, David. The Honourable David Hinton was treasonably broadcasting for and to the Germans.

He broadcast once a week from Berlin during 1940 and 1941; his *'Stimme aus Berlin'* broadcasts became as popular in Germany as J. B. Priestley's were in England.

In 1942 the broadcasts stopped, and Hinton disappeared

from the German scene. British Intelligence learned that Hinton was believed killed in a bombing raid; a report was prepared and the Hinton file was closed.

A secret file was opened, however, in December 1942 when a man purporting to be David Hinton revealed his identity to the British Ambassador in Lisbon, who would never have recognized, in this thin, wasted figure, the young man he'd met at country house parties before the war. The Ambassador concealed Hinton in his private residence while trying to decide what to do with him. 'Hinton is one of us,' he said to his wife, 'we can't just turn him in.'

His wife remembered Anthony Stope-West, who'd lodged with them when he was in Lisbon a few months previously, on some important, hush-hush job. She remembered Anthony had even placed a direct call to Winston Churchill. 'Anthony will know what to do with him,' she said, and the Ambassador sent a coded signal.

Anthony dispatched his personal aide, a lieutenant-colonel, to collect David Hinton, and bring him back in secret to Bedfordshire. After all, David had been his fag at Eton.

'David, you've been a damned fool,' Anthony Stope-West said. 'Now sign this blasted piece of paper and we'll set about getting you into His Majesty's Forces. Then you can go down to my tailor, and get yourself a decent uniform.'

'What regiment are you putting me in, Tony?' David asked.

'I haven't decided yet,' Tony said, 'but it won't be the Lancers. I mean, a chap can only do so much . . .'

Anthony Stope-West's influence extended much further than his rank of brigadier-general would suggest. He was *persona grata* in all the private councils of the Joint Chiefs of Staff of the Allied High Command. It was known he had the ear of the War Cabinet. Many people privately asked why, but no one mentioned it. Not in the hearing of Winston Churchill, anyway.

Basically, Stope-West was a planning coordinator unhampered by conventional chains of command. He was a devious man of complete charm, unassailable on either moral or social grounds.

Someone once said of him that he was a perfect *alter ego*, a voice of conscience that could argue equally well on either side. If a general were squeamish about sending a group of men to certain death, Anthony Stope-West could point to the number of other lives that would be saved; if a general were lenient in his interpretation of a military law, Stope-West could express a moral indignation that would have done credit to an archbishop.

Anthony Stope-West was given a free hand; his brief stated in the most succinct terms, 'do anything to help the Allies win the war'.

When he had learned that Hinton was broadcasting for the Germans, he suspended judgement. After all, David was 'one of us' : he didn't behave badly without a reason. Anthony Stope-West refused to take up an attitude until he had all the facts.

Personally, Stope-West thought that military activity was old-fashioned; the chief weapons of the future, he was convinced, would be psychological. Perhaps there was a way in which British Intelligence could make use of the 'fact' of Hinton's broadcasts for the purposes of psychological warfare.

When he heard that Hinton had gone off the air, he was appalled. So long as David Hinton was in Germany, making his regular broadcasts, a possibility existed that Stope-West might be able to make use of him. It had been no more than an idea. But that idea appeared to be lost when Hinton disappeared. Now Hinton had turned up again. Stope-West, a prudent man at all times, arranged Hinton's posting to his own headquarters.

One day two weeks after David Hinton had been smuggled back into England, Anthony Stope-West was sitting at his desk, reading the reports of the monitoring services at Caversham. These covered the German and Italian radio stations looking for coded messages intended for the many agents the War Office had uncovered and now secretly controlled. These reports were coupled with others from the network of 'correspondents' British Intelligence maintained in Germany. Shuffling the reports together, Stope-West became aware of what at first seemed an insignificant fact : a woman called Heidi Lotl was doing a daily broadcast from Strasbourg that seemed to have achieved immense popularity. The programme was simply called *'Tagesschau'* – a look at the day – but since it had started six months before the tiny broadcasting station at Strasbourg had achieved its best-ever listening figures. Heidi Lotl had become a popular heroine throughout Germany, with the same sort of reputation, Stope-West thought, that Hinton had once enjoyed.

That was when Stope-West saw how he could still make use of Hinton.

David Hinton watched Anthony Stope-West shuffling his papers. He got up and walked across to the window, looked out over the grounds. It all seemed so long ago, yet so close. How could he accept the rank that Anthony Stope-West had achieved; how could he take him seriously? They'd been boys together, had shared the same wild impulses. They'd been invited together, on exeats, to this sort of house, the homes of their contemporaries. This had been the dower house of Sir Bartholomew Wallace's home. He and Tony had come here with young Clarence Wallace, had ridden these fields, cubbing, later hunting. Tony had gone to Cambridge, David to Oxford, but they'd met frequently, in this sort of setting. It seemed natural to be here, but not with someone who called himself 'Brigadier'.

He turned and sat on the sofa near the fireplace. 'Tony,' he said, 'I was just thinking about the old days. That time the groom brought up that horse in a lather and you questioned him and got the truth out of him and then gave him hell. I was awfully impressed with you in those days.'

'I hope you still are...'

'Of course I am. You've been damned fortunate, but you've deserved it. You always knew exactly what you wanted, didn't you? That was always my trouble, I never knew what I wanted. Nobody seemed interested, nobody seemed to give a twopenny damn. I was determined I'd beat them all.'

'You did, in the academic way. . .'

'That wasn't what I wanted. . . I wanted to be superior in other respects. I wanted to be admired, I suppose, for what I was, not for what I could do. You always had a purpose. I remember that quite clearly. Whenever I said, "Oh, bother this, let's cut it", and we'd escape from a tedious prep, I'd be left with nothing to do; but you'd always have an alternative plan. You wanted to escape because you had something better to do. I wanted to escape from purely negative feelings. I suppose it was the same thing with this German business. I saw them as a *Herrenvolk*. I didn't realize you can't drive a tank through a graveyard without knocking down a few headstones.'

'And you came to your senses again, that night the bomb dropped on the house in the Kurfürstendamm . . .?'

'I suppose so, though I didn't know it at the time. . . I'd finished my broadcast that evening and a car took me to the house in the Kurfürstendamm. I was early, but there wasn't time for me to drive out to my place, so they put a suite at my disposal where I could bathe and freshen up. They were giving a reception in my honour and I was to meet a man from the *Kraft durch Freude* campaign. Also the press were going to be there in force. In fact, a press car was parked outside the building when the bomb fell. My car and driver were still there, and he was the one, so I read, who told the press I was inside. After all, he'd seen me go in, hadn't he, and I'd no reason to go out of the back door.'

'So the press were told you'd gone into a building which they watched destroyed, and naturally assumed you were dead.'

'That's right.'

'Exactly where were you and what were you doing when the bomb fell?'

'I'd bathed and had dressed. I was alone in this suite they'd given me.'

'Then the bomb fell?'

'That's right. The building was destroyed.'

15

'Why weren't you killed?'

'How do I know, Tony? All I know is that – well, the first thing I knew was that the wall started to crumble. I hadn't heard a bomb, of course. I just saw the wall start to crumble outwards as if it were made of cheese. And then the air started, sort of rushing about, if you know what I mean, and the curtains came whipping in, and I suppose the air must have sucked me out through the window, which, by the way, I'd opened previously, and the next thing I knew I was outside the building in a garden, about twenty or thirty yards from the building. I was tight-wrapped in an enormous velvet curtain. I got out of the curtain as best I could and then I just wandered away.'

'But surely, someone must have recognized you? Someone must have known you from your pictures in the papers. . .?'

'Well, I suppose not. After all, I was covered in muck and dust, wasn't I. . .?'

'Were you? You tell me. . .'

'Well, of course, I must have been, mustn't I? After all I'd been blown out of a building, through all the rubble and debris of the walls, and across the earth of a garden. . .'

'But you were wrapped in a curtain. . .'

'Not my face. My face was all scratched, and there was blood everywhere. . . I must have had concussion, I suppose.'

Slowly and patiently, Stope-West took Hinton through the story of the bombing : the way he'd holed up only half-conscious in the corner of a derelict house for what he later worked out were two days and nights; the way he'd thought about what he'd been doing, and had decided to escape from Germany, since they must think him dead.

'Sudden decision, wasn't it?'

'Not really. It'd been building up in my mind for some time. National Socialism was easy to believe in 1938-39. Nazism was hard to take, in 1940-41.'

'What decided you, finally?'

'Reading my own obituary. They'd given me the front page, and said I'd been a traitor to England. I realized how much they despised me, even though they'd been prepared to make use of me.'

They kept at it; the escape through Germany, France, Spain, which had taken months. Fortunately, Hinton had money with him when he was blown out of the window and took a chance on passing openly across Germany by train. After all, he had a *laissez-passer* signed by Dr Goebbels himself, in his German cover name. By now his face was puffy and the cuts had become infected; he was quite certain his features were unrecognizable. 'Allergy', he had explained to suspicious guards along the way.

In France he collapsed and luckily was picked up by the Resistance, who smuggled him, almost unconscious, down the escape route. He was taken into a monastery at Perpignan where they tended his cuts and cured his fever, before shipping him, by night again, across the Spanish escape route, into Portugal. Once in Portugal, getting to Lisbon had been easy.

'And all that time, you never told anyone your English name . . . ?'

'David Hinton, the traitor, the *"Stimme aus Berlin"*, was reported dead. I wanted it to stay that way until I got back to England. . .'

'Where they'd most probably shoot you as a traitor. . .'

'I didn't know that. But if I had known it, I wouldn't have cared.'

Stope-West looked at him. That much he could believe. There'd always been a fatalistic streak in David Hinton, even at school. He'd been a rebel, in the days when only one child in a hundred cared to rebel; he'd been punished over and over again, but always had accepted his fate. In one sense it was almost as if he'd wanted to be punished. Just as when he walked into Portugal? Had he wanted to die?

Again Stope-West wondered what sort of man David was, beneath it all. Could he be relied upon? Did he have the strength of will to do what Stope-West wanted? Was he, perhaps, a German double agent? So far, of course, he'd had no opportunity to make any contacts, but could the brigadier trust him outside Headquarters?

'Why did you make those broadcasts, David?' he asked.

David stretched himself, before talking as if reciting the two-times-tables he'd learned by heart. 'I believed in National Socialism. I believed in Hitler and the Germans at first. I didn't like what was happening in England. I came to hate our policies. I didn't feel particularly British – I was more at home in Berlin than ever I had been in London.'

'And now?'

'Don't misunderstand me, Anthony. It's not that I like the British more; it's just that I approve of what the Germans are doing less. I didn't know how long I'd have been able to go on making those broadcasts without something of my real feelings showing through. I think Himmler was already on to my changed attitudes; he had me watched all the time. But luckily, though I never actually met him in person, Adolf liked me and in a sense I was under his personal protection.'

'And that didn't bother you . . . ?'

'Why should it? Look, Anthony? you're a dyed-in-the-wool Royalist. I'm not. In another time and another place I'd have followed Cromwell, I suppose.'

'You're not going to tell me you're a communist . . . ?'

'I'm not any kind of an "ist"! I try to look at individual situations, that exist in a particular moment of time. In 1938-39 I didn't have much time for what was going on in England. What men did we have who were dynamic enough to take the country forward? Not one. And the bloody Jews were taking the country over. . .'

'That much at least has stuck to you. . .'

'What?'

'Anti-semitism. . .'

'There you go with your "ists", and your "isms", again. I'm not anti-semitic. Not as a general policy. It just seemed to me that specific and particular Jews were working to take the country over.'

'And now . . . ?'

'Now I despair. When I see the bloody shambles old Winston Churchill has gathered around himself to fight the war, the second-rate lot of nincompoops. . . Let's face it, Anthony, in the old days we wouldn't have let that lot come out of the black hall...'

Anthony Stope-West laughed. He himself had little respect for the Chiefs of Staff. Mountbatten was all right, he supposed. Winston himself was all right. But some of the career officers...

Now David had the sly look that Anthony Stope-West knew so well, had seen so many times when they were boys together.

'They can't be up to much, if they need to make you a brigadier...' David said.

'Well, David, you can thank your lucky stars I *am* a brigadier, or God knows where you'd be right now. Possibly in front of a firing squad.'

'All right. What plans have you worked out for me? Something Machiavellian, I'll be bound.'

'You're going to make another broadcast, David,' Anthony said. 'This time from Strasbourg on a programme called *"Tagesschau"*, run by a woman called Heidi Lotl. She broadcasts every evening, and all Germany tunes in to her. The *"Stimme aus Berlin"* will come to life again, for one broadcast only. But this time, I shall be writing the script.'

CHAPTER TWO

They picked me up one Saturday afternoon in Morecambe. I was an instructor at the Officer Cadet Training Unit, Heysham, at what formerly had been a seaside holiday camp. This Saturday I'd arranged to be off duty; I'd designs on a NAAFI girl known to all as 'gin and easy'.

I felt rotten because I only wanted one thing from her: quick, complete, and uncomplicated sex. I booked a double room at the Hydro Hotel, Morecambe. The proprietress was used to thirty-six-hour romance. 'War's a terrible thing,' she said. 'It keeps loved ones apart.' She gave us a front bedroom as her contribution to the war effort.

The NAAFI girl and I were sitting on a sofa in the window bay drinking gin and lime; I hate the stuff but kept pace with her. She talked incessantly; didn't I agree it was her duty to make life as agreeable as possible for the brave men who were giving everything to win the war?

I had said 'yes', when the knock came on the door, and a male voice with a rap like a woodpecker said, 'Captain Colson, sir?'

She went into the bathroom; I put the gin bottle, the lime juice, and the glasses into the bottom of the empty wardrobe to hide the traces of our bacchanalia, and opened the door.

A company sergeant-major of the Military Police was standing in the passage, with a private who looked like his sparring partner. The sergeant-major's arm whipped up in the sort of salute a typewriter would make, a clacking carriage-return motion that placed his finger on upper case a tenth of an inch from the neb of his peaked cap.

'Captain Colson, sir?'

'Yes, Sergeant-Major . . .?'

He beckoned to the private, who dug into the small leather pouch on his belt and extracted one letter and a pad. He took a pencil from his top-pocket, handed me the letter, the pad, and the pencil together. The envelope carried my name and a tally number; I licked the indelible pencil and wrote my signature next to the number on his pad. He tore off the carbon copy and handed it to me, then put the pad and the pencil away, as if defying me to get them from him.

It was a brown envelope. The address carried my number, rank, name, address at Heysham and the ominous code 'OU Top Secret', stamped on front and back. It was sealed with a number in green wax, and crossed with red lines.

I started to go back into the room but when I tried to close the door on them, the sergeant-major put out his hand.

'Not alone in there, are we, sir?' he said.

I stepped out into the corridor, drew the door closed behind me, and glared at him. He retreated three paces with the messenger. I broke the seal and opened the envelope. The instruction it contained was signed by Brigadier Stope-

West. The message was uncomplicated. Captain Colson will report to this office immediately. With the instruction was a letter with an unrepeatable system of codes, and a short message which specified that anyone to whom I might show the authorization was commanded, and authorized in the name of the King, to give me any facility I required to speed my progress to London. Clipped to the authorization was a first-class travel warrant for the LNER or the LMS, and a twenty-four-hour ration card.

I put the papers back into the envelope and beckoned to the sergeant-major. 'Right, Sergeant-Major, I've just got a few things to do here, and I'll be back at camp in an hour and a half, in plenty of time to catch the four-fifty.'

He looked me straight in the eye. 'The brigadier's adjutant had a word with me on the telephone, sir, and I'm holding the two-twenty in Morecambe station for you.'

'But I haven't packed, Sergeant-Major.' I would still have time for half an hour in bed.

'Your batman's on his way to the station, sir, with an overnight bag and your shaving equipment.'

'I'll just go and ...'

'Private Wilkinson could say goodbye for you, sir; the adjutant was most specific.'

I opened the door and glanced back into the room. She'd got into bed. All her clothes were on the chair beside the bed. The gin had done its job. She pouted languorously. But I grabbed my cap and stick from the chest of drawers, and drew the door shut behind me as I went out.

'All yours, Private Wilkinson,' I said.

The proprietress was smirking in the foyer. 'Duty calls, eh, Captain?'

'Wait ten minutes, then send somebody upstairs with a tray of tea and a couple of buttered crumpets,' I told her. 'And tell 'em not to bother to knock. The lady's hard of hearing.'

Brigadier Stope-West's unit occupied a stately home in Bedfordshire. They stopped the train at the local halt, just for me. A car was waiting, a lumbering, dark-green Humber that still smelled of shot-gun cartridges and pheasants, chicken sandwiches and port, county virgins and gum-boots. It was driven by a lady of fifty who'd brought her lavender bags to war with her. Her voice sounded like purple velvet and she used the adjective 'jolly' about fifty times between the station and the porticoed front door. As I climbed from the car she put her hand on my arm.

'Don't let them bully you, young man,' she said, and then she touched the peak of her cap, her eyes twinkling. 'Permission to carry on, sir?'

I saluted her and, despite the fortune on her fingers, murmured, 'Carry on, Private.' As I marched up the steps the touch of her hand was still warm on my arm.

When I announced my name to the sergeant sitting behind the bare-topped trestle table just inside the door, he leaped to his feet, saluted, and bellowed, 'Private Tompson!' Private Tompson appeared from what had probably been the Boot Room.

'Take this gentleman to Captain Arkwright,' the sergeant bellowed. I later learned this was his normal voice though, at the time, I assumed Private Tompson was stone deaf. He might have been; he was about seventy years old. Together we waddled along the corridor, over what seemed like miles of Army haircord carpet.

This was the administration centre. I whistled through it on a cloud of names and ranks, hand-shakes and best-of-luck-goodbyes. The officers, in ascending rank, had many things in common – manicured fingernails, Savile Row uniforms, pink cheeks.

It was a relief to emerge at the other end relatively unscathed.

The brigadier occupied the dower house, tucked away beside a lake, far from the common herd. He was dressed in brown whipcord trousers and a dark green shirt with silk froth at the throat, and was much younger than I'd expected. I would not have been surprised if he'd produced a cigarette holder, sat at a piano, and sung to me about 'lilacs in the spring'.

'Had a good journey? Trains are hell, these days, aren't they? Did they get you a seat?'

I sat down, exhausted. It seemed the correct condition to be in.

'Care for a drink? One of these coffin-nails?' The cigarette case, a slim gold box, contained Woodbines one side, Craven A the other.

I pulled out a pastilles tin, worn smooth in my pocket. 'I get mine by post from Rothmans,' I said. His eyes gleamed.

'I say . . . Do you really . . .? Could I possibly . . .?'

I offered the tin to him. Well, hadn't the old ducks said don't let them bully you?

When we were both sitting he opened a green cartridge-paper folder on the table in front of him.

'How's Morecambe?' he asked.

'It's a job. . .'

'How's your wound?'

'Which one . . .?'

'The one in your head.'

I'd escaped from Holland in an open boat; on the way home the over-eager Polish Squadron had gunned me, killing my sergeant, and putting me in Stoke Mandeville where the boffins who practised on the burned faces of the RAF aircrews reshaped my forehead.

'It's all right.'

'Not still getting headaches, are you?'

I laughed. I'd been a bit wild for a time, knowing I'd got myself through Holland and then been snookered by our own forces. Three trick cyclists had played inside my skull for three months to stop me wanting to murder every Pole I ever saw. They'd had a partial success; I still hated them, but I was content to let them kill themselves.

'No, no headaches. So far as I know, I'm quite fit again.'

'Sea air obviously agrees with you.'

'Good as a holiday.'

He looked briefly at the green folder then closed it. 'German still all right?'

'So far as I know.'

23

'French . . . ?'

'Not in gin . . .'

He laughed. 'Kept your sense of humour. . .' Then the smile went from his face as if wiped by a blackboard sponge. 'You'll need that,' he said. 'I'm dropping you over France tomorrow.'

For a moment I couldn't comprehend what he'd said. You don't do things that way. At least, the Army doesn't. 'Dropping you over France tomorrow', as if I were a sack of fertilizer. What about the briefing; what about selecting the men; what about the training, the vital coordination of visual signs . . . ?

'Give you a brief outline,' he said, 'then we'll have a chat about it. We've been training a team. Your old lot, Special Services.'

I felt like a man who sees a one-time, still-loved mistress across a crowded room, and hope flickers again.

'Know Castleford?' he asked.

'The place?'

'No, the man. Major Castleford.' He chuckled. 'Would you believe it, Major Castleford has a temperature of a hundred and four. Tonsillitis, so the quack says.'

That didn't surprise me. Training officers spent a lot of time sipping pink gin in a warm mess; it's no preparation for skulking in wet hedgerows.

'He ought to have 'em out,' I said, knowing what was to come.

'You're the logical choice,' the brigadier said. 'You speak French and German fluently. You're an explosives wallah, and you know the drill. You'll have seven men trained by Major Castleford, and you can't have a better recommendation than that.'

'There's a sergeant-major?'

'Of course. Sergeant-Major Williams. I believe you know him?'

'We've worked together. . .'

'Yes.' He paused, sipping his gin as if he'd invented a new flavour and wasn't sure I'd approve. Finally he looked at me. 'I come of an old cavalry family, you understand?' he said.

I did understand.

'It may sound old-fashioned, but I believe that if we can't beat the Germans without descending to their levels of physical brutality, there's not too much hope for the country.'

'Point taken, sir.' My way of saying 'old-fashioned bigot'.

'It's a volunteer job. . .' he said.

'I thought it would be when I saw that train waiting for me on Morecambe station. . .'

'My adjutant tends to dramatize sometimes, I think. You had supper?'

'My batman packed a few sandwiches.'

'God, man, you must be starving. Come and have a bite. I don't eat in the mess; it tends to get a bit crowded. . .'

We ate in his quarters, in a window bay overlooking the estate. The meal was served by his batman and a borrowed mess waiter; the tablecloth and the napkins were white linen, the cut glassware sparkled. 'You don't mind?' he said, when we had been served with casserole of pheasant, and were drinking a '37 Beaujolais, as he switched off the lights and drew back the curtain. It was a bright, moonlit night, and the gardens and fields below us were flooded with light. In the distance a searchlight stabbed at the sky, wavering round and round looking for a target. Nothing else moved in the landscape below us, or if it moved, it did so unseen.

'England's a tangible reality to me, you know,' he said. 'I have the advantage that many of these abstract ideas of loyalty, and patriotism, and honour to one's family are realities as tangible to me as the stone of our house, the hide of our horses, the long line of my ancestry. Does that seem nonsense to you? Does it make me an old-fashioned relic of the past?'

'No, sir. It's something I know nothing about and therefore I don't form opinions.'

'That's remarkably forbearing of you. But what I'm trying to say is that I couldn't bring myself to do your job. I can't do anything by stealth.'

'You feel obliged to throw down a gauntlet . . .'

'That very act was symbolic of everything I feel. You issue your challenge. You forewarn your enemy of what you intend and do it to the best of your ability...'

'By Queensberry rules...?'

'That's the idea!'

A plane had been caught in the cone of the searchlight, which now followed it across the sky. We could see the explosion of the ack-ack fire, hear the staccato crackle of the skin-piercing fragments, and once again I felt my flesh tighten. I'd ridden a plane through that stuff and knew how it felt to see pepper-pot holes appear in the fuselage all around you.

The brigadier closed the curtains and put the lights back on. 'Making for Bedford, I expect,' he said.

I cleared my throat. 'Permission to speak, Brigadier?' I said.

'That means you're going to say something difficult. Are you going to tell me you won't go...?'

'Brigadier, you don't need to tell me these things. But it's part of your code, isn't it? You're saying to me, "I'm asking you to go, but I feel obliged to tell you that, if our positions were reversed. I wouldn't go". It's all part of the code, never ask a man to do anything you couldn't do yourself.'

His face broke into a smile of such an inner warmth that I could not bring myself, at that moment, to dislike him. I had a reputation for a hatred of authority, an independent I-will-not-be-disciplined bloody-mindedness. And here I was, framing excuses for a stiff-upper-lip brigadier, putting words into his mouth that would excuse him.

Let's face it, I didn't have any of his patriotic feelings. England just happened to be the place where my mother dropped me. That was why, as a boy, I'd gone on the thumb all the way round Europe, picking up languages without any of the British arrogance that makes it effete to be able to talk to the natives in their own lingo. Lowly lads didn't start wars; they said '*voulez-vous coucher avec moi*' and got on with it. It was his war, not mine. And now he was asking me to volunteer for something he, by birth, breeding, tradition and instinct, could not do. But the bugger was smart; no wonder they kept him in a job for which, on the surface, he would seem to be unsuited. Lead by inspiration and example, the good book said. 'An Officer should be at the front of his men.' A junior officer, that is. Senior officers were allowed to sit back at base with a telephone and a soda-syphon.

We didn't observe such distinctions of seniority. Any officer in Special Services fought in the middle of his men, neither in front nor behind. He couldn't do that, and he was telling me so. He couldn't even eat in the mess with the up-from-the ranks officers because it got 'too crowded'. But the bugger was smart. He'd disarmed me completely by telling me so, by his free, frank and voluntary confession of inadequacy. I wondered how many other men he'd sent on impossible jobs that way?

'Okay,' I said, deliberately using the slang as a mark of my low-bred vulgarity. 'I'll do it. Now you'd better tell me, sir, just what the it is.'

They were on parade and waiting for me when I arrived at Naseby, scene of ancient battles and modern training. The Special Services had taken over a large house which stood in the centre of two thousand acres of rolling pasture land.

I recognized Sergeant-Major Dai Williams at once but none of the seven men he had standing at attention beside him. I walked along the rank, looking at each man in turn. Dai must have briefed them; as I came level each man spat out his name, but didn't mess about with his rank or number. I didn't give a damn what rank a man thought he held; that was for the pay-office. So far as I was concerned, any job had one commander, one second-in-command, and a number of specialists.

Even on first acquaintance, I didn't take to David Hinton. He was over six feet, too tall for a parachutist, and had the lean aristocratic look of his class. Also he drawled, and that annoyed the hell out of me, each consonant clearly articulated in the public school manner, the vowels long, the nose high.

'Right,' I said. 'I won't waste any time. Major Castleford

is unable to take this mission, and I'm going in his place. We leave in thirty-six hours, and in that time, I'm going to get to know every one of you. Until we leave, we'll spend all our time together.'

They hadn't eaten breakfast; we took it together round a large, circular table that could have been made for King Arthur, and probably was by the feel of it; each man told his tale.

Jim had dealt in antiques, the sort you find in attics in Fulham, not New Bond Street. He lived in a flat in West London, usually on his own. Sometimes a girl would move in with him, but usually left when his drunken wife came shouting for an increase in her alimony.

Tony the Greek owned a fish-and-chip shop in Camden Town. He wasn't a mainland Greek; he came from Cyprus and wanted to distinguish himself from the Turks. Ambition : to stop frying fish and start a café, or a restaurant specializing in meat and two veg. Reason for joining Special Services? More pay, more leave, more chance to fiddle.

Frank Goldberg was the son of a tailor, destined to spend his life cross-legged, making suits. Greenberg had an almost identical biography and ambition and I guessed that, if they both survived, they'd set up shop and home together. Reason for joining Special Services? Hitler. Hitler personally, not Hitler as a symbol. I didn't like that. Hate's a bad and unreliable source of inspiration and energy; almost as bad as love.

John interested me greatly. He was a typical product of the London slums. He'd been a pimp, bookie's runner, con man, name it and if it was sleazy enough, at some time or other he'd done it to survive. He'd volunteered for Special Services by mistake; he thought he was putting down his name for posting as a batman and had visions of regular employment for his team of lovelies, servicing the Officers' Mess. When he got in he enjoyed being treated as a man by other men; to his astonishment he could do all the physical things that were required of him and his training-officer had the sense to realize that here was a man with one unteachable talent, the ability to survive under any circumstances.

Five feet ten, and weighed only eight stone in uniform. Not a speck of fat on him. Where could he have got fat? Face like a skull, with skin on it. But he had a sense of humour.

Jack was a parson; he defrocked himself at the start of the war saying, 'God's in abeyance', and went out to fight the good fight in his own way. He broke his nose at Dunkirk, volunteered for the Air Force when he got home and was going to Canada to be taught how to fly when a pack of U-boats blasted the boat off the water. Jack arrived back in Glasgow after he'd been afloat on an improvised raft for sixty days and nights.

The brigadier told me he'd thought for a long time about giving David Hinton a cover name, but decided in the long run it would be dangerous to send a man in with the handicap of a name to which he wouldn't automatically respond. No one in the troop appeared to have connected this David Hinton with the man who'd been doing the broadcasts. But, what the hell if they did? They were all under orders.

To take the pressure off himself and God, Jack turned to David. 'Why did you join this mob?' he asked.

Long pause. Hinton knew I knew, but we had to play charades. The rest of them had the right to expect that David Hinton was there for a valid reason. The strength of a chain is the strength of its weakest link, and all that rubbish.

'It seemed the right thing to do at the time,' he drawled. 'Like buying a horse, marrying the right sort of gel, or putting a fiver in the plate at Christmas.'

'You been on any jobs?' John asked him. All eyes were focused on him, and for once David Hinton was in a club without a membership card.

'Not yet, but I'm quite looking forward to this one. It should be fun,' he said.

I winced. 'Forget it, mate,' John said. 'It's no bloody joyride.'

David Hinton flushed with anger. The brigadier had given him a cover story but Hinton was only capable of being himself. John looked at me as if to say, 'you must be out of your mind even to think of taking him with us'. I knew we had no alternative. We'd rub some of the corners off him.

I got them to tell me what jobs they'd done, what specialist training they'd had, what roles they thought they could best fulfil.

'This job is basically one of movement. We have to get somewhere. I shan't tell you where, not just yet. When we get there some of us have to do something, and I shan't tell you what just yet either. Then, with luck, we get out.'

'And that's where the trouble starts, eh, sir?' Jack asked.

'You've got it. Getting in will be easy. Doing the job, will also be easy. But getting out will either be easy or absolute bloody hell.'

I watched them through the routines of training : they were tough, agile, and very fast. As I found out to my cost. We were standing at ease for a few minutes, getting our breath back. I walked along the rank, slowly, idly. When I'd passed John suddenly I whirled around and tried to hit him in the gut. It would have put him on his back if I'd connected. I didn't. He spun like a ballet dancer or a bull fighter, lifted his arm, and chopped me across the muscle. My arm felt as if someone had just put a .45 round into it with a dum-dum head.

'Sorry, sir,' he said. But then he smiled; I smiled, they all smiled and I knew we'd get on. They were testing me just as I had been testing them, and I had passed.

The whole of the day we sweated together, going through the obstacles on the course, climbing the frames, stripping weapons and assembling them again, defusing mines and booby traps, setting mines and booby traps, throwing knives, firing arrows from steel bows, moving silently and unobserved across the pasture, through the shrubs, along the edge of the drive of the house.

I checked each man : all had been given Tet-Tox and TAB injections, anticholera, smallpox inoculations well enough in advance for them to have recovered.

All had passed the trick cyclist, though he reported finding evidence of tension in David Hinton and Jack. 'Dammit,' I told him, 'we're all tense. I'd be worried if we weren't.'

Supper was ended, the mess waiters cleared the table, and all the lads sat back and let them do it, unused to being waited on. I asked the mess-corporal to bring in a bottle of whisky, and nine glasses. Hinton told him to not to forget the soda syphon, as if the mess-corporal were his life-time batman.

'If you must ruin the whisky with soda, David . . .' I said. 'Corporal, would you show Private Hinton where you keep the soda syphons?'

I'll give Hinton credit for imperturbability. He rose to his feet, went outside and procured a soda syphon which he put on a tray. He whipped a napkin across his arm : 'Anyone else care for soda?' he asked, making a round of the table. I could see Dai was nearly pissing himself laughing, but I can take a joke and the tension needed relaxing.

Quite a card, this Hinton. Man of mercurial moods. Lot of character, lots of spirit. But how would he show on the old-fashioned but still very necessary basics, like obedience, personal courage, loyalty to the rest of us? I had doubts.

I put them aside. We had a lot to do. The plan I had to outline was thin as parson's porridge, and I knew damned well they'd recognize that fact.

He lurched to his feet, sweat pouring down his face despite the ice-cold interior of the plane. Sweat on his chin and on the end of his nose, his face covered by an oily sheen. I thought he intended to make his way to the latrine behind the brown Army blanket suspended from the roof at the rear of the Dakota, but when he was standing upright he clutched at the stanchion which ran across the plane, missed it as the plane banked, and fell to the steel floor.

We were over the Channel and air pockets were playing havoc with our flight path and our guts. When he lifted his head I saw the cut on the side of his face where he had caught one of the rivet heads. Blood was beginning to well, staining the oily sweat like a bloodshot eye. He started to get up but the plane dipped again, then rose, flattening him back on the deck with a short jab that made him grunt. He didn't try again, but crawled on all-fours like a beaten dog. When he was in front of me he lifted his head level with my knees but didn't touch me. He looked up.

'I can't do it, Captain,' he said.

Either he'd jump, or we'd throw him out. It's a damned messy way to start, throwing out one of the men. Many times the only reason a stick of men will jump is because each man believes no other man will refuse the jump. I couldn't risk them all refusing because one man wouldn't jump. Especially if that man was Hinton. Of course, I ought to have known he'd never pluck up the courage for an 'operational' jump. Practising is easy; tally-ho, and over the top, and all that sort of crap. But this was the real thing. We were jumping into the unknown, and a thousand rifles could be pointing at us, and for that you need real guts. What the hell, what was there to be afraid of? Either your parachute opened or it didn't. If it didn't, you were in for a quick death. If it did, you still had to land. Sometimes you broke a knee, or an ankle, put a hip out of joint, or waltzed into a tree and a branch stuck up your arse, or hit the roof of a building and cut yourself to ribbons on the slates, or landed across an electric wire and fried.

'Hinton,' I said, 'there's nothing to be afraid of. . .'

'I won't be able to do it, Captain,' he said.

I'd had it all before. Time and time again.

'Captain,' he said, 'I really can't do it. I can't.'

'When that red light comes on and we open that door you'll stand up. When the light stops winking you will clip your line to the bar. When the green light comes on, you'll walk down the plane with the rest of us and when your turn comes YOU . . . WILL . . . JUMP. Because, if you don't, I personally will knock you unconscious and throw you out, and, unconscious, I wouldn't give you one chance in a hundred of landing properly. IS . . . THAT . . . UNDERSTOOD?'

The red light had come on and started to wink.

I went to the front of the cabin and slid back the door. It came easily. Air rushed in, biting, slicing, rushing wind, cold as clouds. I hitched my static cord clip to the rail.

Quick look round. They're all right. With one exception. We need him, unfortunately. Jim leading; we don't need *him* because Tony the Greek, following him, has trained to replace Jim, if necessary. Freddie and Frank next, both

Germans by ancestry though born and bred in Scunthorpe. Then John and Jack.

The red light flicks a long time. Twit of a navigator slides his rule and gives us a twenty mile alert. Damn him. It takes thirty seconds to hook a stick of men. Jock Stapleton once jumped trousers down when the green caught him on the bog. Sergeant-Major Williams, five feet ten of iron, rubs the heel of his hand; a look at Hinton is enough. Hinton is a snot-nose and the sergeant-major doesn't trust him. But we've no replacement.

Red steady. Quick glance. All hooked. Green still out, only seconds left. 'Our Father which art in Heaven', we hope. Damned funny if, up there, He's backing the Krauts. They say, '*Vater Unser...*'

Green on. Jim's out good. Tony. Freddie. Frank's good going out but the slipstream's flipped him and he'll have to work. John's good. Jack's good but too eager. Now the Right Horrible. Lips working. Sweat running off him like an Irish beer-drinker's piss. Left hand out, right hand. Christ on the Cross. He'll jam the bloody doorway. Raise my hand to chop, he anticipates and ducks. Onto my knee. We've done this before, mate. Ready, steady, Dai chops both Hinton's arms on the muscles. Leg between Hinton's legs, thigh under Hinton's crotch, lever forward, oopla and out. Dai swings out, easy as off a Cardiff bus. I follow him.

The stick spreads out below and in front of me. Count 'em. Good. All opened. That's a relief, grab the lines and spill air from the back to slant the descent. The sergeant-major is doing the same thing and I pray we don't catch a thermal and do a hands, knees, and boomps-a-daisy. Already we're below Hinton. Earth spreads below but I wouldn't say a patchwork quilt. Quilts are soft with mother's love.

Platoons of vine fields, neat lines at first, but as you go down the vines close together towards the horizon and open apart below you, so it looks as if waves are rippling across the landscape. No roofs, thank God, a bastard to land on. No telegraph poles, and that's good, because, up here, you can't tell the difference between a cold telephone wire and a hot power cable. Ground flattens where I'm aiming, rolling grass land. Bail out air to steer myself near the hedge; less distance to run if tracer starts spitting. Nothing coming upwards; good. When puff balls fly, fragmentation casings seek out your lower parts with only serge to protect them. No tin jock-straps for parachutists.

Trees rush up, a hedge like a thin knife blade; the wind swings me mercifully into the field and the flat mass below suddenly sprouts green blades; down, over, roll, up, ears singing, snap the harness latch, stand and drag lines to hold the billowing folds of the parachute and think – ought to bring a shopping bag to put it in – but keep on pulling to crumple the silk into a ball.

A figure steps from the hedge, into the moonlight where I can see him – and he can see I have my hands full of cords. Mind's a camera, snap, print, enlarge. He's about forty, prematurely grey. Dark suit and a roll neck. Beret on his head.

Things are wrong. Beret doesn't fit him. Army jackboots.

He's carrying a light machine-gun. He thrusts it forward, dead steady, pointing at an aching void in the pit of my stomach.

'Welcome to France, Captain Colson,' he says, in English.

'Welcome to France,' the man repeats, as if expecting an answer. He is smiling; beneath that ill-fitting beret it looks like the grimace of a brothel-keeper. He starts to walk forward. Watch and wait; a walking man's unstable, balances on one foot at a time. And he is holding the machine-gun forward clear of his body, his arms slightly extended. How many times have I told my lads, don't extend your arms, but hold the butt of the machine-gun against the side of your body, lock it there. Machine-guns kick upwards, don't they? That's what I've always taught my lads. Now is my chance to prove it the hard way, isn't it? Wait till his foot starts to rise, then move. I dive forward and down, tucking my head well in, forward roll. The barrel drops but not far or quick enough, and I tuck my head and shoulder in and when I come up my line has changed to the side. When he pulls the trigger the gun kicks as I expect and the bullets stitch a line in the ground going past me and away and he starts to pivot on the one foot in my direction but I've rolled again with my left shoulder tucked in this time and I come up under him, under the barrel of the kicking gun with my crossed hands forwards so they catch the gun barrel and lift it up and out of his hands, and I turn and kick sideways with the edge of my boot in the bottom of his guts and jerk on the machine-gun barrel and he goes off the end of it, backwards over and down and I jab forward and hit him under his ear with the butt of his gun and he flattens out and down. I reverse the gun, turn round looking for more of 'em.

My lads had all been balling their chutes when the firing started; now they were belly flat on the ground and I was looking into the barrels of their pistols. I jerked the machine-gun upwards and as if drawn by strings they half rose from the grass and scuttled into the hedge on each side of me. Even Hinton ran.

No words of command, nothing said. It was a situation to which their training had accustomed them.

The man in the beret was coming round. It's a bad blow to take the butt of a rifle under your ear and the side of a boot in your gut. I knew. I'd had it time and time again, and not always in training. Jack was our first-aid wallah, crouched beside the man in the beret feeling his heart and pulse, lifting the lids of his eyes. He turned to me.

'He's all right, sir,' he said.

I was already going through the man's pockets, but not expecting to find anything. A couple of pieces of paper on which columns of figures had been added, bills from some café or restaurant, I should imagine. A handkerchief with a black border a centimetre wide all round it. So you lost somebody. Too bad; we'll send the handkerchief back somewhere – if we ever know where and to whom to send it. Nothing else. Nothing else? No keys, no diary, address book, money or wallet and, most significantly, no identity card or military pay-book.

A Nobody? From Nowhere? Even on a job we carried a

pay-book. We were issued with a new one for each job, containing name and number. No unit address. No rank. No page for military skills or achievements so the Germans wouldn't know you'd trained in radio, or explosives, or were a sniper, or had a language qualification. But this man had nothing.

He was coming round slowly and Jack looked at me. 'He'll be all right,' he said again, as if he needed to reassure me I hadn't killed him. Jack still cared about such things; a lot of parson was still hidden beneath that active and sometimes brutal exterior. 'He'll have a large bruise, and a headache.'

'He's lucky. He could have a hole in him.'

The man in the beret looked at me as his eyes opened. Already they were in focus, but I'd known he was fully conscious several seconds before he opened his eyes.

'*Merde*, you're quick,' he said.

'*Merde*, I have to be.'

He smiled, but the movement of his facial muscles must have pulled the bruised area and the smile turned to grimace. 'You also hit hard,' he said.

'Again, I have to.'

His English had a Maurice Chevalier accent to it.

'*Qui va sur chasse ...*'

'*Perd sa place,*' he said.

'Okay, so you've read a little French ...'

'*Merde*, I am a little French.'

'A little? What's the rest?'

'German. I come from Alsace ...'

'So does stuffed goose liver.'

'I was born in Alsace. My parents were German.'

'That's why they let you in the German Army? Because your parents were German?'

'I was never in the German Army.'

'You were never in the French Army, either?'

'That's true ...'

'Mary had a little lamb. Its fleece was ...'

'Yellow with purple spots ...'

'So you know the password. Who told you?'

36

'Avalon.'

'Why the gun . . . ?'

'The Germans bring over parachutists and drop them, thinking we'll believe them to be English and talk to them, even perhaps introduce them into The Line.'

'Why don't you carry an identity card?'

'In case you are Germans. . .'

'Where did you get the machine-gun?'

'Avalon.'

Four days ago we dropped a courier in advance with a radio. The Germans had been waiting for him, too. He escaped, but the Germans caught Avalon. He was the leader of the local Resistance, such as it was, and they took him into the prison outside Sarreguemines from which no one had ever escaped. Near the Franco-German border, it was the local headquarters of the Gestapo. Our courier had gone to ground in St Avold and had radio instructions to stay away from us. But last night I'd been at the end of the line when he sent his last message.

'Where is Avalon?'

It was a trick question. Only the Gestapo knew the answer to that one.

'He's disappeared.'

'I'll tell you where he is. He's dead. The Germans killed him three days ago, in Sarreguemines. . .'

Tears came to his eyes and that convinced me. You have to peel an onion to get tears out that quickly. Or love someone.

'Il était mon père . . .'

'And the handkerchief?'

'Ma mère – morts, tous les deux . . .'

I believed him.

He helped us stuff our parachutes into the bottom of the hedgerow, squashing them into the debris of fallen leaves along the bottom of the ditch. The parachute silk was soft and springy and we had to jump on them to hold them down while we shovelled wet leaf-mould over them with our hands.

Four men out watching, Dai and me and the Frenchman

37

keeping ourselves well back in the bushes, but feeling as exposed as a Punch and Judy show, waiting for the sharp teeth of the crocodile to snap at us.

The Germans must have seen us come down; we'd chosen the area carefully and the German defences were concentrated five kilometres away; we couldn't hope to arrive unseen but by the time the Germans arrived, we hoped to be well hidden. We had dropped on the shoulders of a valley between Ittenheim and Achenheim; we set off due east, farther up into the range of hills, the tall evergreens of Alsace. It was country I knew very well; I'd tramped over it as a boy, moving parallel with the Rhine. Our final destination was the town of Strasbourg on the other side of the mountain that rose in front of us, due east, but mercifully on this side of the Rhine. Saverne, known from its strategic location historically as the 'Eye of Alsace', lay to our left; behind and to our right were the vine-covered slopes at the start of the 'Wine Road' I had travelled with such unconcern, a mere few years before, a rucksack on my back, a few francs in my pocket, and a young man's thirst in me for new sights and experiences.

Now the Germans occupied Strasbourg as of right; they'd always claimed Alsace anyway as German territory, and were busy infiltrating the countyside. Frenchmen were sent away to Germany to work in forced-labour camps and hopefully to die; their farms were being taken over by good Germans from the east. Labour was mostly Polish prisoners; this time the Germans intended that the character and nature of the people of Alsace would be destroyed from within, on the age-old principles of conquer and divide, divide and rule.

We formed a file, with the Frenchman leading and Dai in the rear, and made our way up a track into the trees. The track had been cut at some time by a mountain stream; now it was dry and had been roughly levelled by the passage of farm carts. We'd travelled a half-mile when we saw the lights of a German patrol ahead of us, and had scant time to hide beneath the pine-fringed woods before the first troops were upon us. They came past pushing bicycles, walking

38

their machines doubtless to avoid even the slight noise of cranking pedals. They moved silently and were obviously well trained; I blessed our good fortune that, with typical Teutonic inflexibility, they had not thought to turn off their lights. The headlamps were taped, of course, and in each tape was cut the shape of a cross; they'd appeared as so many fireflies in the darkness of the night. I hadn't anticipated bicycles and could have been caught out by the speed of their arrival. We lay in the bottom of the trees, motionless. I counted twenty men under the command of an *Oberleutnant*.

When they had gone I signalled to my men to stay down. Another patrol, six men without bicycles, with machineguns held at the ready, was following the first, ready for the incautious to leap out of cover. I chuckled. They'd have a long wait for me making that sort of mistake. Dai Williams was lying beside me, another old hand at this game. He put his mouth close to my ear and spoke, sucking in his breath while he talked so his voice would not be projected.

'That the lot, Captain?'

'First lot on bicycles; second lot no bicycles but just behind 'em. How? Where's the transport?'

We waited. Five minutes passed. Ten. Fifteen. Out there. Somebody. Who? How many? Night sounds carry. I could hear the occasional traffic on the road from Strasbourg to Ittenheim. Main road, leads to Saverne. No main road to Achenheim, but I could still hear vehicles on the secondary road. Moutain ahead, full of noises. Pines are long and thin and the leaves are sharp and play staccato music at night. Pine needle carpets are soft, but they still crunch if you listen, every time a rabbit or a hare decides to move. Strasbourg, five kilometres away, rumbled in the night like a baker's stomach. Couple of planes droned over, travelling low and slow.

I hated being holed up this way. At the start of a job. The adrenalin was still pumping from the parachute drop; I wanted to be up and away. I could sense the same feeling in the men; they wanted to cover ground, put distance between themselves and the dropping zone. Several of them had looked at me as if to say 'what's he waiting for?' But discipline held. The Frenchman was impatient. We had a long way to go. He jerked his thumb to indicate we should be on our way, but I shook my head. My hearing was better than his. Motor bicycles, coming slowly up the track, hoping to carry off the prisoners their passengers would take. Four. Each with a side-car. Dog in each side-car with a handler, all went past without a sideways glance. Large Alsatians. What other breed of dog would you use in Alsace? Bloody fools. The stink of petrol and monoxide fumes from the exhausts of those bikes would deaden a tracking dog's sensitive nostrils for at least half an hour. Riding there like regimental mascots on parade. Looking neither left nor right, searching ahead. The dogs ought to have been dismounted, and with the second patrol.

When the bikes had gone past, we went deeper into the wood and circled round the path, relieved at last to be on the move. A stream ahead ran down the hill-side across our path. There we divided. I sent Hinton straight across. They'd never believe it. They'd pick up his scent and leap the stream, but they wouldn't believe we hadn't used the stream to put the dogs off the scent. John and Jack, left turn on the banks of the stream this side, Frank and Freddie right. That'd confuse them. Which way should they go, straight over, left or right? Assuming the dogs had recovered their sense of smell by that time. Me in the stream with Jim; Dai in the stream with Tony; left and right. Then figures-of-eight up and down the stream, in and out for half a mile. All out of the stream at the point where Hinton had crossed and straight along the track. The dogs and the men with them would go out of their minds following such a pattern.

Another mile along the small track we'd taken we came to a labour camp, in which Poles lived, or so we'd been informed, lived when not cutting pit props for the mines of the Saar. The Germans were starving the Poles, and we'd been told the camp was completely self-contained. We smelled it from a quarter of a mile. We left the track to skirt the camp; several camp dogs set up howling when, despite the odour all around them, they got a whiff of us; we were close enough to hear the German guards cursing them, telling them to be quiet. The camp would have been told by telephone that parachutists were in the district, and that the regular troops were hunting them; I couldn't see the camp guards leaving the warmth of their huts to do soldiers' work. We didn't see a sign of the Polish workers; doubtless they were locked up in their long, low barrack huts for the night. Plumes of smoke came from each hut; at least they'd have wood stoves to keep them warm, burning the pine tree off-cuts. The camp was enclosed in a triple-strand, barbed-wire fence; a dog was running round inside one of the wires and he clawed at the strands, barking furiously in our direction. A light came on at the top of a timber tower at one corner of the camp, and it swung slowly round the perimeter. We were out of its range. We went ahead in arrow formation. The Frenchman led us, with Dai now by his side. John and Jack, and Jim and Tony the Greek, were watching the flanks. Hinton was in the centre where I could keep my eye on him. Frank and Freddie were behind him so they could do the same. We were equipped with the US M1 Garand rifle I preferred. Its range is farther than that of the Thompson, the ammunition is lighter to carry, the rate of fire is slower but the aim is more accurate, and being a semi-automatic it can't waste its bullets in a spray. Each of us also had a Webley pistol, a Colt .45 automatic, an Army-issue knife with a six-inch, double-sided blade that snapped off at the handle if you weren't careful, and a piano-wire garotte. Down the seams of our trousers we carried a bow in three sections, with arrows down the other seam. I could hit a cigarette card at fifty feet, a postage stamp at ten feet, and the impact would carry the arrow over an inch into a plank of wood. If you cared to waste your time aiming at planks of wood. Under the collar of my jumping jacket I carried a one-sided Ever Ready razor blade, and a chain looped in my cuff that screwed and locked to form a spike eight inches long. Five ampoules of morphine in my field-dressing pocket, each with its own needle and skin swab, though when the pain hit you, you weren't thinking of skin hygiene. Six high-energy, compressed beef cubes with the morphine; and in my map pocket a plastic box that contained an ounce of Cut Golden Bar and rice papers, a dozen barley-sugar-twists, unwrapped, and the equivalent of £250 in French, Spanish, and Portuguese money. The middle button of my trouser fly was a compass; the insoles of my Innsbruckers folded out to reveal a map printed on silk; the stitches of my left cuff were set out in a random transfer letter code, a copy of which was on Stope-West's desk.

CHAPTER THREE

When we came within sight of Strasbourg, the Frenchman led us into a copse in a fold of the low hills. Pine trees behind us, vines along the slope to left and right. 'This is a good position,' he said; 'we discussed it and thought you'd be safe here.' Then he left us, as arranged.

We watched him go swiftly through the vines and over the hill below its crest; he moved well. Then we changed our position. I didn't like that – 'we discussed it'. The less people who knew where we were, the better. Anyway, his responsibility had been to watch us come down and run interference if the Germans were at the dropping zone, and then bring us to within sight of our objective; now the urban *maquis* would take us over. We moved a kilometre south, near the crest of a hill. It wasn't such an obvious place.

The night was cold. Bombs were dropped on the Rhine port beyond the town and as we ate cold bacon and drank soup from tins we watched the firework display. The German ack-ack defences in the Siegfried Line shot down two Lancasters and we watched one glide past us in flames; a man baled out about ten kilometres south of us; I hoped he'd quickly get away. He had his own method of getting home. I'd brought a lightweight sleeping bag a boffin had invented; two thin bags of nylon sealed airtight together. You crawled into the inner bag and blew into a tube. It worked a treat until you needed to get out in a hurry, though the air caused you to wobble disconcertingly every time you turned over. I preferred the hard earth, but I wouldn't say so in my equipment report.

Jack sat with his back against a tree. A cold night. It would be a long one. Earlier there had been clouds and a half moon that wiggled through them like a silver fish escaping from the deep. Now, no clouds, only an infinity of twinkling stars. Freddie and Frank on watch, the rest asleep. Tony and Jim on their sides, back to back; Captain Colson and the sergeant-major on their backs; John, restless in his sleeping bag, no doubt dreaming; Hinton awake, moving restlessly.

Back on the raft. Alone, on a mercury sea at night, moonlight streaking across the still water as if he could dip in his arm and it would come out silvered. They say you go mad; that was the first thought he'd had when he'd come to, that dawn, alone on his raft. They say you go mad, from the loneliness. 'The Lord is my Shepherd, I shall not want.' How often the thought of those green pastures had sustained him. He could have done with having his head anointed with oil. His skin cracked, his lips cracked, and for days he raved and hallucinated. Until the miracle happened. The rain. He would always be convinced the rain was an act of Divine Intervention, a miracle. He gathered the rain in his shirt, sipping each drop, sometimes letting it collect until he had a spoonful, sometimes with his mouth open beneath the cone, catching the water which dripped through. 'Yea, though I walk through the valley of the shadow of death, I'll fear no evil.'

Freddie woke Tony and Jim; they were instantly alert and went to take their turn on guard. Freddie and Frank slithered into sleeping bags. Hinton got out of his sleeping bag and stretched cautiously then, seeing Jack with his back against a tree, he crawled over and sat beside him.

'You ought to be asleep,' Hinton said, his voice a whisper that only Jack could have heard.

'So ought you.'

'We have a lot to do tomorrow.'

'That's why we both ought to be asleep.'

43

There was an intimacy about being together in the night, but Jack didn't want to talk.

'I am curious why a priest should join this mob,' Hinton whispered. He obviously *did* want to talk.

Jack sighed. To keep silent, not to answer, would be a deliberate snub. 'I consider myself a soldier, not a priest.'

'Eye for an eye, eh? Smiting your enemies.'

'Something like that. Anyway, what about you? You're a more unlikely candidate for this lot than I am. . .'

'Like Washington, I labour to keep alive in my breast that little spark of celestial fire called conscience . . .'

' "Oh, conscience that does make cowards of us all." '

'No, it's not conscience so much as nationality. I wear my nationality, like a widow's weeds, reluctantly, in sorrow, and for as short a time as possible. I can talk to you, you know. You have some notion of what I'm driving at.'

'I suppose it's the cloth that does it : the great levellers, we are prepared to sup with peasants and princes.'

'I wasn't thinking of you as a parson . . .'

'If not, you're the first one who hasn't.'

Jack lowered himself down in his sleeping bag, brought its fold around his ears. Hinton watched him sadly and then drew back into the undergrowth, not wishing to see the stars any more.

When Tony came off guard, he lay down in the centre of the circle. He liked to look up at the night-time sky, but sleep rapidly closed his eyes.

Sergeant-Major Williams woke me just after five, by waving a tin of hot tomato soup under my nose. That, too, was a new invention; a tin with two lids; you took off the first lid to reveal a fuse; touch that with the end of a glowing cigarette and you could be drinking boiling hot soup in seven seconds flat. Unless a sniper saw the glow of the cigarette end. The soup was so hot it scalded my mouth. Sergeant-Major Williams squatted down beside me, talked again in that breath-sucking way that prevented his voice carrying.

'Sorry about the tea, Captain. I didn't want to authorize a fire, even smokeless,'

'Quite right, Dai, but I wish they'd make that fuse a bit shorter, this damned stuff's scalded my mouth.'

'You properly awake now, Captain?'

'Yes, I think so . . . Why?'

'Don't look up. Carry on drinking your soup.'

'Germans about . . .?'

'No. Not that. . .'

'Then what the hell's wrong . . .?'

'Don't hardly know how to tell you. . .'

'Then come straight out with it, man.'

'During the night, somebody's stabbed Tony the Greek in the back.'

'Dead?'

'As mutton.'

'You heard nothing?'

'Not a crack. But all the same, somebody knifed him in the back. . .'

'Anti-social.'

'Jokes, sir. . . He's dead.'

'Smile, dammit. Three of 'em could be watching us.'

He smiled. At least, I think he did.

'Nobody knows you know?' I asked him.

'No, sir.'

'Don't say anything about it.'

Quick look round. We'd been there six hours. Everyone would have taken a turn at guard, except Hinton and me. We were saving ourselves for bigger and better things. Freddie and Frank together, Jim and Tony, John and Jack. If Tony had kipped between Freddie and Frank, he must have climbed into the sack while they were on the ground asleep. I couldn't imagine them coming off duty and settling down on opposite sides of a sleeping figure. That meant John and Jack were on guard, supposedly, when whoever knifed Tony did it. But in our guard pattern the men got into position facing each other across the camp site, each looking beyond the other. It was done that way for a purpose.

If two men on guard face outwards, away from each other, one man may be knocked out by a crawling German; and the other knows nothing about it if his back's turned.

The Germans move as quietly as we do when they have to. Our way, a man will see anyone trying to crawl up behind his mate, and he is able to cover him. And both of 'em are watching the camp between 'em. Nobody could crawl across our camp site and stab Tony the Greek with two men looking across it. Just not possible.

'On your own?' I asked the sergeant-major.

'When?'

'When you mounted guard.'

'Yes. I took two o'clock to three o'clock.'

That's the worst spell in the middle of the night. Grey ghosts walk out of bushes, scuttle through the shrubs at you. Not enough sleep before or after. Damp in your bones, and your eyes hard to focus.

'That could have been when they knifed Tony.'

'I've already worked that out, sir. I'll never forgive myself.'

This was no time for brooding. Cold morning, grey with mist, a grey morning curtain that in London would have been a yellow, lung-collapsing cloud of acid. This mist would burn off by seven, and leave the morning clear and crisp. And, we hoped, the road busy with people since we intended to move. Tony wouldn't be moving. You'd think he was asleep, one arm beneath his head, the other inside the sleeping bag, his body flat, the way it has to be if you're comfortable, lying on the hard ground. Or dead.

Ships that pass in the night. Another soldier I'd never got to know. There were too many. Suddenly I shivered, there in the morning mist.

'Could someone have come into the camp site while you were on guard?'

'I'll guarantee they didn't. That's not what I meant when I said I'd never forgive myself.' The sergeant-major was the best I knew at unseen movement; he could make it himself, detect it in others. Crossing ground unseen is either impossible or easy. Depending on the feel you have for a piece of terrain. How low you can get your body, how skilfully you can blend in with every tiny dimple. What gives people away is unnecessary movement, movement between movements. Watch a snake; absolutely still, moves fast, then goes

46

absolutely still again. No one could have come into that camp site undetected while he was on guard, even though he was on his own. What did they all say – he had eyes up his arse, and in the back of his head. ..

'So, it's one of us?'

'Yes.'

'Any theories?'

'Hinton!'

'That's prejudice. Anything happened during training? Before I joined you?'

He shook his head. 'Tony was a quiet lad. Gave offence to nobody. Good trainee, well above average. But kept strictly to himself. I can't think of any reason anybody'd want to get even with him.'

'Could be two of 'em together, of course.'

'John and Jack?'

'Can't see that combination.' The pimp and the parson? Too unlikely.

'What shall we do with Tony, sir?'

'Get Freddie and Frank to dig a hole and bury him.'

'Very good, sir.'

'Get his pay-book, his discs, escape money, and morphine.'

'What about his ammo?'

'Leave his ammo. We're carrying enough. You could get his tobacco and his compass. And his barley-sugars . . .'

'Nothing else?'

'Any handkerchiefs he's brought. I forgot to pack any . . .'

I watched while they buried him. It didn't take long – when you think what a good man he'd been.

CHAPTER FOUR

Dai Williams and I left the rest of them and walked down the sparsely-wooded slopes towards the road that runs from the south-west into Strasbourg. We stopped just before the road in a small coppice to change our outer clothes by the simple expedient of taking them off and turning them inside out. What had been khaki battledress became a smock and trousers of wash-bleached blue cotton twills, identical to the ones workers wear all over Europe. Dai's had been bleached more than mine and looked lighter. My green beret became black, our jumping smocks soiled gabardine rain-coats, apparently double breasted, fastened with four buttons and belted. Mine was sand-coloured; his navy-blue, topped by a greasy-banded trilby. Two minutes' work with a small screwdriver and I had stripped the Innsbruckers from my boots. With a thin undersole, they looked as civilian as I hoped I did. The finishing touch was a battered cardboard attaché case I'd brought in my rucksack folded flat; it had the seedy, edges-frayed look of a lifetime of union meetings. Dai carried a paper parcel, and a walking stick.

Cars and horse-drawn wagons ran along the road. An Army section bowled along in three lorries, horn-blasting the wagons and the civilians into the side of the road. Bleary-eyed soldiers returned cold from a night on heat. Workers, slowly pushing bicycles, as if to Calvary, Army combinations, staff cars, a constant stream thin as grey bile. Finally our stretch of the road was empty and we stepped out, moving towards Strasbourg, two more artisans or clerks or minor functionaries, going to work. Head down, shoulders forward, back bent, feet shuffling. Today is a day like yesterday.

No one showed any interest in us. Why should they? We looked no different from the rest of the workers.

Soon we arrived at the outskirts of the town, and the density of the traffic grew. When we had crossed over the first tributary of the Ill, we cut left until we came to a bridge beneath railway lines. Here the streets were wider, with sheds and warehouses. The few houses rose five storeys, but with a plain, sand-coloured exterior, not the white-washed and timber, cross-hatched façades I could remember as typical of this region. We passed several workers' cafés and restaurants before we came to the *Deux Elèves*, the Two Scholars. It was thronged with people, none of whom appeared to have seen the inside of a college.

We went in. Ordered *deux blancs*. No one seemed to pay

any attention. Men standing at the bar, which was covered in corroded zinc. Not many bottles in the holders behind the bar. No hard-boiled eggs on the counter. I dipped my finger in the wine and sucked it. *Pas mal*. Dai said nothing; he could never completely obliterate the Welsh sing-song of his native tongue. Oddly enough his French came out like Marseillais. Mine was okay. I'm a natural mimic. All tongues are alike to me. Let me listen to two men talking for ten minutes in any dialect of any language and, even though I can't understand a word they are saying, I'll give you a faultless imitation of the sound they're making. It was my party piece before the war.

We took our glasses away from the counter to avoid the jostling. No soldiers in the bar. A couple of women, or what once had passed for women. All manner of dialects. Lots of east German sounds, the thin, talk-on-the-teeth, semi-lisp of Poland and East Prussia. Behind the counter a mirror, striped with brown paper. I looked in it, checking faces, physiognomies. Not many Alsatians. Maybe a couple. The rest Germans, Poles, an Italian. The patron was big and fat, but handled his bottles deftly, making a juggling act of every glassful he poured. Strange. Fat men aren't often exhibitionists. This one was uncertain of himself. Was he the true patron? Or planted there by the Gestapo? A lorry stopped outside the café, farting dirty exhaust smoke. The men standing in the back of the lorry shouted with disgust at the driver. They carried long-handled shovels as if they were rifles. When the lorry stopped they threw the shovels down, clattering. Before the war, working men respected the tools of their trade.

A man in the corner. Was he watching me? Five feet ten, crisp, grizzzled, grey hair. Workman's overalls just like mine, wash-bleached, blue cotton twill. Black beret, greasy at the front with sweat so it shined lighter. Watching me? Our eyes met. He didn't look away. I winked. He winked back. International Brotherhood of Labour. A look that said 'us and them'. The hands holding his glass were wrong. Too neat and clean. A clerk's fingernails. My hands and Dai's were dirty. I'd seen to that. He could be a clerk? Work a clean machine on a production line? It isn't all spanners and dirt.

When the men in the lorry had thrown their shovels into a pile, they leaped over the side and came into the café in a thirsty phalanx. An unofficial stop, no doubt, on the way to a construction job. Fifteen *verres du blanc. Attention, bien sec, eh?*

'I don't know where you normally drink, but *chez moi*, the *blanc* is always *très sec*,' the patron said, giving us Act Two of his juggling performance. The men snatched up the glasses and gulped the drink. The foreman, section leader, boss, whatever he was, came from the cab of the lorry and into the café. '*Allons-y*,' he shouted above the hubbub, '*allons-y*.'

Pale Hands *was* watching me, I thought. That was the second time he'd raised an empty glass to his lips. Dai bent his head close.

'Maybe he fancies you, sir,' he whispered, sucking in.

'You've noticed, have you?'

'Couldn't hardly miss it, could I?'

Pale Hands put his empty glass down on the counter top. Then he started to push his way through the crowd towards me, towards us. Damn. I ought to have left Dai outside. Or better still, we ought both to have come in, but not together. Quick look around. They don't usually work alone. Which are the others? No one paying attention. I slipped the knife out of my sleeve and palmed it. Dai moved away from me. One to go in front, the other to catch from behind.

Pale Hands stood in front of me, his eyes looking into my face. Then he spoke. In German. 'Are you not, surely, you are, it is Karl Friedman, from Wissembourg? You remember me, Otto. Otto Kniepach . . . ?'

Hand slightly forward, handle in the palm of my hand, blade up my sleeve, clear the blade, clear it fast. It's damned impossible to hold a knife this way and strike forward. What do you do, hold the blade? Your only hope is to twist your wrist at the last minute, spin slightly to the side, and strike half backwards. But it's messy and complicated.

'Was that your sister?' I asked. 'Maria, didn't she, I mean, hadn't she got, a little lamb . . . ?'

'Maria? Sister? Little lamb . . .? *Nein, Nein.* I am Otto. Otto Kniepach.'

'I'm sorry. I have never been to Wissembourg. I don't think I know you. . .'

It was his turn to look confused. 'I could have sworn you were Karl Friedman,' he said, shaking his head. He turned and left the café, shaking his head as if I'd stolen something from him, something quite irreplaceable. A few of the workmen from the lorry were gathered in the doorway, prolonging the moment of freedom, and he was obliged to push through them.

The foreman was shooing his men out of the café. 'Come on, *allons-y.*'

A man was watching us. A man with a wall-eye. Standing at the bottom of the bar. Had the phoney Otto stopped to speak to me merely to identify me for the other man? Had I been 'fingered', as they used to say in those 1940 James Cagney films? Wall-eye was watching. Quite openly. Watching the foreman trying to get his men to drink the last drops of wine, watching the patron with his juggling act, watching me and Dai, standing there together without talking. The trouble was, I couldn't tell exactly where he was looking at any one time, since both his eyes seemed to point to different directions. Was he looking at me, or the bar, at the foreman or at Dai, at the door or the window?

Looking out, I could see 'Otto' walking down the long street still shaking his head. Nothing remarkable about him. Going neither fast nor slow. It was time for Dai and me to get out of there. Or to try. I had started to touch Dai Williams's arm when the workers going back out to the lorry swirled around us, pushing and shoving good-naturedly. Their foreman, among them, whispered urgently to me, '*Allons-y!* Come on,' and we were swept out of the café, across the pavement, and up onto the back of the lorry before anyone could see we had gone. The lorry started and raced away up the road as though it was being chased, or it was late for work. The foreman had jumped on the back with us, and he handed us each a long-handled shovel.

'*Bonjour,*' he said, '*Je m'appelle François.* Mairie hard er leetul larm . . .'

It took me half a minute to realize he was saying our password greeting. 'No, I say that,' I said. 'You're supposed to tell me what colour its fleece was. . .'

'*Merde* . . . Either yellow with purple spottings, or purple with yellow spottings. . .'

I shook his hand. 'Bit of a bore, aren't they?'

'*Comment?*'

'Passwords. *Très ennuyeux . . .*'

'*Oui, mais bien nécessaire . . .*' He seemed offended I had offered a criticism of 'the system'. It had worked well so far. But the fact is, I get nervous when things go too well. I hadn't been told exactly how contact would be made and that café pick-up had gone too well, too smoothly.

'Where are we going?'

'To blow up a bridge.'

'Openly, like this?'

'Can you suggest a better way? We have a night-time curfew. *Très dangereux.* So, we fool them by travelling openly during the day.'

I looked about me. Now that I saw them more closely, I realized this was an odd crew. No one man was young, or perfectly fit. The foreman saw me eyeing them. 'Quite an army, eh?' he said smiling. 'Czeslaw, here. He's a Pole. He has fits, or so the Germans think. Henk, here, a Dutchman. Works nights in the telephone exchange. Vital war work. He's the only one with a real work-card. The rest are all forgeries. He only has one leg. We hide explosives in the other. We all have job-cards. Also ration-cards, and identity-cards, and *laissez-passers.* This truck has papers. *Ministère des Travaux Publiques.* Bomb damage. One of our men works the petrol pump. Who suspects a salvage squad? We can go anywhere. We can go to places that even a Wehrmacht major cannot go. And all official.'

'And us?'

'We have papers for you, too. You brought the photographs?'

'Yes.'

'Good. We'll stop in a couple of minutes and get your *cartes d'identité*.'

It was a hair-raising drive, through the back of the railway section. The driver made himself conspicuous, barging ahead of even military traffic. Mostly they let him, sometimes blew their horns angrily at him. We were jolted from side to side, but somehow, standing conspicuously in the open truck with a long-handled shovel beside me, I felt totally concealed.

The lorry stopped briefly outside a printing shop. A man had been waiting in the doorway. François had put our photographs into an envelope and threw it on the pavement. As the lorry carried on down the street I saw the man bend and pick up the envelope. We did a circuit of the building, and were back outside the shop in five minutes. The man was standing there again. The lorry didn't even stop as it went past him. A moment later the window into the cab opened and François was handed an envelope. Our *cartes d'identité* were inside, complete with photographs and the official stamp.

Next stop, the Parc des Ouvriers. Part of Strasbourg's history. Twenty acres, flower-planted, with long narrow lawns and benches, a couple of cafés, tables for picnics, and the Oestermann House, built in 1470 of pink granite, with a steep angle and sloping tile roof. Before the war it housed the Museum of Artifacts. Now it was used as the central transmitting station for Radio Strasbourg and contained a studio with its own control room, a main control room for the dozen or more other studios dotted about the city, and the transmitting section, with an aerial built onto the roof. The Oestermann House even had its own emergency supply of electricity from a generating station built underground.

The studio itself was small; the only programme which used it regularly was 'Tagesschau'.

Next stop was on the Avenue Miramée. An involuntary stop when a German half-track blocked the street. The man sitting next to the driver climbed out when he saw our lorry behind him, and sauntered back. He was the equivalent of a sergeant of the Military Police except that he carried a machine-gun. Four men in the back of the half-track, and a

Spandau machine-gun mounted just forward of the half-track's tailboard. As the sergeant walked towards us, the gun swung in a lazy arc, covering him and the street. *'Attention,'* François said, but we all carried on talking as we had been.

The sergeant halted at the window and methodically asked for papers. For the truck and the driver. The driver produced them equally methodically, from a clip-board. The sergeant read each one, handed it back. Then he walked slowly round the truck as if he were examining tyre pressures. When he was back beside the driver, suddenly he pointed at the back of the truck with the muzzle of the machine-gun. It seemed to be pointing at Dai.

'Papers,' the Sergeant said, flatly.

Dai leaned forward, produced his papers from his inside pocket, including the newly-made *carte d'identité*. If the gum had not dried. . . Dammit, of all the people there, he would chance to pick Dai. . . If the ink of the forged stamp was still wet . . . if the photograph looked too new. The sergeant looked at the papers, looked up at Dai, back to the paper's particulars. Something was wrong. We could sense it. Knife down in my hand. The half-track was ten yards away. A long throw. Dai would go for the sergeant, leaving the gunner to me.

'Where are you from?' the sergeant asked, his loud voice harsh, his German the staccato hardness of the Berliner.

Dai looked at François; François waved his hands in the air, and Dai waved back at him. It was a masterly performance, an imitation of deaf and dumb speech. Then Dai took another piece of paper from his pocket and handed it down to the sergeant, who took it without speaking, opened and read it – a discharge report from the military hospital in Colmar, attesting that the bearer, Albert Trevinnal, was being discharged from the French Army on the grounds of having been rendered deaf and dumb by bomb blast. He bundled all the papers together into the folded *carte d'identité* and handed them back. I tucked the knife back up my sleeve and wiped the sweat off my upper lip. The sergeant turned and went back to the half-track. The Spandau didn't move, covering him. The half-track moved slowly forward, then accelerated away down the street.

We followed the route taken by the half-track for a while before we turned off. This was a site-inspection tour, a look on the ground at our several objectives. My hands itched to be doing something active, but first I had to look at the reality, compare it with the aerial photographs and the descriptions I had been given. I'd left enough to chance, taking over someone else's mission. This much I intended to see for myself. François couldn't complain; I approved six of his locations out of eight; not a bad average when you consider we hadn't yet told him exactly what we intended to do.

CHAPTER FIVE

I didn't like the feeling of the camp site when Dai and I returned. There had been an argument, that much I could tell. I'd left Jack in charge; Freddie and Frank, the two F's as I'd begun to think of them, were on guard. Hinton was reading a book. 'Stupid bastard,' I said and snatched the book from him. Just what we needed, an English book to give us away. He held out his hand. The book was in German, published in Berlin. I threw it back at him.

'Had to do something to pass the time away, while you and the sergeant-major was cavorting in Strasbourg. . .' he said. I short-arm jabbed him and he went down backwards.

He knew why I'd hit him. So did the others. This was one mission I was going to carry out on a basis of minimum information. I was the only one who knew all the details, and intended to keep it that way. Then, if one of them was taken, he couldn't give the whole game away. If one of them became separated from the main party, just too bad.

'Anything happened?' I asked Jack.

He shook his head. *Something was wrong.*

'You talked about Tony?' They looked at each other, uncomfortable. So that was it. Who killed cock robin?

But something else was bothering Jack; a departure from procedure.

'Why didn't you tell us to move camp?' Jack asked.

'Because there was no point. We'll be moving camp after dark, just in case the sergeant-major and me were spotted.'

'What if whoever killed Tony had decided to come back?'

I called Freddie and Frank in off guard, then sat them all round in a ring so they could look across our heads and outwards. The sergeant-major and I sat in the middle of the ring. Hinton came and sat with us, as if by right, until I put him back on the perimeter.

'Whoever killed Tony couldn't come back,' I said, when I had settled them, 'because he's been here all the time. One of you killed him. The sergeant-major and I both know that.'

My accusation brought no surprise to them, called out no burst of hot denial.

The evening sky was darkening, and purple shadows reached long fingers stealthily across the terrain in front of us. Night would soon be on us, night and dark concealment.

'I don't know why anyone should murder Tony; all I can guess is that whoever it was did it because of something that happened during training before I joined you. One thing is quite certain. I'm going to go on with the job as if nothing had happened. We'll be short-handed without Tony, but the job's still possible. It'll still be possible if you all kill each other, except Hinton. I intend to spend my time and energy carrying out this job, which means keeping myself, the sergeant-major and Hinton alive. Each of you had better look after himself.'

The murmur started, each one talking to the others quietly, none of them talking to me. It was bad for morale to isolate the sergeant-major, Hinton and myself in that way, to show the others how 'dispensable' they were. No man likes to believe he's personally unnecessary. But we'd established a killing method, and Tony the Greek had been its first victim. We'd devalued human life back there in training and

56

couldn't complain if killing seemed an acceptable way out of a dilemma, however small, however inconsequential.

At Morecambe I once took a session for the Army Bureau of Current Affairs, when you let the men smoke for an hour and put their feet up. A list of titles was supplied 'for possible discussion' and stipulated, 'the leader of any session should make no attempt to deliver a speech or a lecture, but should merely use the title as a starting point for conversation'. The title I'd chosen was – 'you can do anything with a bayonet, except sit on it'. It would have been a good subject for discussion right here, outside Strasbourg.

Night had crept slowly onto us, a damp cold blanket that seemed to suck the heat from our bodies. I shivered. We'd taught these men to kill, and in the process had given one of them a reason for doing it. This was a move across a psychological chess table. You do this and we'll do that and you'll do this, with no one ever being bold enough to predict which piece would achieve the check-mate. But I'd accepted to do this job on certain terms, and the very acceptance had compromised me.

I'd agreed in advance that, if necessary, I'd kill a woman. I won't say an innocent woman; she was a part of the German war machine I'd joined the Army to help destroy.

As soon as the sky became completely black with no stars visible, no moon, we moved to another hill-top from which we could see the first. Just in case we had been followed, and they decided to attack. Jim had brought a radio. An American job that worked off dry batteries. It was the first I'd ever seen. We turned it on at seven o'clock, and I listened on headphones to the Strasbourg station. Clear as a bell.

They'd given up the pretence of it being a French station. No more *'Ici Strasbourg'*, and bright French music. *'Hier ist der Deutsche Rundfunk'*. Five seconds' pause, presumably so that the other stations could join the network. Then the music. Stirring march music for about twenty seconds, faded down for a voice superimposition. The one word, *'Tagesschau'*, then the theme music, a light tune full of violin runs that had probably been specially composed. It gave me an image, so to speak, of Heidi Lotl herself, a forewarning of

57

her, like perfume scented at the opening of a door. Ten seconds, fade again, another superimposition, and then *'Es spricht Heidi Lotl'*.

Her voice was warm and immediately compelling; she began simply but with confidence. 'Good evening, all my listeners, wherever you may be, and thank you for coming to hear me. Today has been another day of victory for us all . . .' And then she went on to give a list of German successes, in news form, but lacking the matter-of-fact tedium of a normal radio pronouncement. I was watching the dial of my watch, keeping an exact check on her timings. At exactly 19.03.15, Heidi Lotl introduced – 'My Distinguished Guest for this evening, a soldier, recently returned from service at the Russian Front'. She made it sound, inadvertently I am sure, as if he had returned to her arms. Name, rank, and number. And then a personal account of what it had 'really' been like, a 'true-to-life' description of the fighting at the front. He implied, rather than stated, how brave his comrades had been. He deplored, rather than condemned, the animal brutality of the Russians, seeming almost to regret the inescapable truth that the world would be a better place without them. It was a sincere performance. As I listened to him, I could feel the icy fingers of the Russian cold gripping my heart, but then, suddenly, I must have begun to smile.

The sergeant-major saw me. He lifted one of my earphones to listen. 'Telling jokes?' he asked. No, they weren't telling jokes, but the brave soldier from the front had suddenly revealed the source of his 'inspiration' to me. What he actually said, was, 'I saw him in the sights of my rifle, so close. So close I could see the cartridges, like fine, zinc teeth, sharp, with the sharpness of grief, and death . . .'

The devil. He'd lifted that. And, what's more, from an English poet, Wilfred Owen. *Arms and the Boy.* 'Let the boy try along this bayonet blade how cold steel is, and keen with hunger of blood . . .' He might have been a genuine soldier from the front, his detail about mess tins and slops for food and fear of artillery was authentic enough, but his script had been written in the Department of Psychological

Warfare, and he'd been rehearsed in his poetic ad-libs until he was word-and-pause perfect. Fine, zinc teeth, indeed! But I had to admire his performance.

At 19.13.15, they gave one minute of music, presumably to allow Heidi and her listeners to wipe the tears from their eyes. He'd ended with another quotation, though for the life of me I couldn't pin it down. 'I go back, tomorrow, perhaps tomorrow to die, but I'd rather die, small and good, than live grand and evil. Thank you for listening to me. Goodnight.' Fade in music. Swelling organ chords.

In England it would have been a voice, soaring into 'I know that my Redeemer liveth'.

The German played Wagner. On the organ.

I wasn't interested any more. The Celebrity Spot. Just the way I'd heard it in England, 19.03.15 to 19.13.15. Ten whole minutes. But I'd had to check they hadn't changed the programme format, even though it meant wasting valuable battery time.

Suppertime. Bacon, on a long strip. Mind you take off the interleaved toilet paper that never comes away whole and always sticks in your teeth. Christmas pud to follow. Jam in the top of the tin seeps through the thick doughy mass while you're cooking it in a billy of water over a smokeless cube that smells to hell of formaldehyde. Powdered tea, sugar and milk all in one tin. The milk, never completely dissolved, joins the paper in between your teeth. A barley-sugar stirred in helps the sweetness but plays hell with the colour, turning it to soldier-grey. Everybody silent, thinking. Everybody guessing. Who's the killer? I didn't want to know. Didn't want anyone to tell me. If they told me, I'd have to do something about it. This was no place to take a Summary of Evidence, hold a court martial.

Somebody didn't want Tony the Greek to survive. Simple as that. I didn't want any man who stood between David Hinton and that broadcast to survive, simple as that.

Time for a last briefing. All done on time. 'Synchronize watches' really meant something. At 18.00.00 hours you will do this. Eighteen hours, no minutes, and no seconds. You've all seen the aerial photographs, you know exactly who, what, when, where, and how. Don't ask me why, that's not my department. Plan A. If everything goes according to plan. Plan B, if you have to depart from Plan A. Plan C, if Plan B won't work. Flexibility. It had to work.

'You don't think whoever killed Tony might be a traitor?' Hinton asked me.

'This isn't the Eton bloody Wall Game. If he's a traitor, he doesn't know all the plan, does he? Why run the risk of exposing himself here and now, instead of waiting until we're on the job? It doesn't make sense.'

'Tony could have found the traitor . . .?'

'And was threatening to tell the Headmaster about him? If Tony had found a traitor he'd have stuck his knife as far as possible up the traitor's arse.'

'Must you be so disgustingly coarse, sir?'

There it was again, that 'get-back-behind-the-green-baize-door' contempt. He was right.

'No, you're right. I needn't be so coarse. I don't think the traitor theory is any good. A private grudge. More or less. And I don't want to waste time or energy on it.'

'You may need to . . .'

'Then I will, *then*. Not now.'

Hinton and I left together. Down the hill again. Along the road again, but this time in the dark. Holding the side of the road, ready to leap into the ditch if necessary. It wasn't. The curfew wasn't until nine o'clock. Hinton moved well, and fast. We walked together and talked. To make us seem more natural and in German, of course.

'What did you think of Major Castleford?' I asked.

'Not much,' Hinton said.

'He has a high reputation. . .'

'So has Montgomery, and I don't care much for him, either.'

'Can you tell me why?'

'Montgomery, or Castleford?'

'Castleford. I don't give a shit about Montgomery. . .'

'You can be coarse in German, too?'

'I can be coarse in any language.'

'Castleford had that in common with you. A low-bred vulgarity that revealed itself only when he wanted to destroy something or somebody. You're quite appallingly vulgar with me because you want to defile me. It's an expression of your own inadequacy.'

'Psychology, too?'

'Physically, Major Castleford was in good shape. Quick mind, I'll grant you, quick as a greyhound. But what good is a greyhound's mind when it can be trained to chase a mechanical hare? Ideal chap for my friend the brigadier. Just like you. Tell you where the enemy is, show you how to get there, give you the other greyhounds to chase with you, and off you go, happy as sandboys.'

Ouch, that hurt. 'What about *your* lot? Chasing after foxes, shooting pheasants ...'

'That's not the point. You hunt a fox to kill it, to prevent it eating chickens. You shoot a pheasant to eat it yourself. . .'

'To give you the strength to go out and hunt more foxes . . .?'

He ignored me. 'But you chase a mechanical hare for the thrill, no more, no less.'

'Major Castleford hated the Germans. The greyhound doesn't hate the hare. . .'

'Major Castleford had highly-developed survival instincts. Without that, he couldn't have generated the hatred. . . One thing distinguishes your class from mine. We have no survival instincts. That's been the ruination of the British aristocracy.'

'Thank you for informing me.'

'Don't make cheap remarks, sir. You've a right to know. After this war's over, you'll become the aristocracy. The chaps who are what they are because of what they can do. No bunkum about heredity. Unless the jerry-builders, the property speculators, the armaments manufacturers squeeze both of us out.'

'Is that why you broadcast for the Germans? Or did they hold a gun to your back?'

'My friend the brigadier isn't holding a gun in your back right now, is he? Coercion has many forms.'

'So you were coerced?'

'I never said that. Now shut up, sir. Here's a German patrol. Theoretically, we should be scared stiff by them. They like that. They wouldn't like being ignored, so give them one of your sickly smiles, sir.'

The patrol was marching. Ten men. A one, four twos, and another one, at the back. Greatcoats, jackboots, steel helmets, packs, water bottles, small packs. Rifles slung over their shoulders and my guess was they didn't have one up the spout. No bayonets. I produced a sickly smile by reflecting on Hinton's opinion of me. I drew behind Hinton to give them more room to pass. Good man, a grenade in his left hand; right hand in his pocket, doubtless clutching his Colt .45, with one up the spout. Where am I going to jump if anything happens? In the ditch? Left, right. Right's better, I can run along it, get well away before they load. Why weren't they in a truck? Where could they be going this near to town without a truck?

Suddenly I realized what they were, why they had no bayonets. They were a squad of what we call 'Jankers' in England. Men being punished for petty military offences. Fall in outside the guardroom when the rest of them are in the *Kantina* enjoying the music and the show, or out with the girls, and march from A to B. Then turn round and march back again. When they'd gone I drew level with David Hinton. 'All the King's horses, all the King's men, marched up the hill and marched back again. . . How are you working that grenade?'

'On a wire, up my arm.'

Bloody hell. One jerk and the pin comes out. . . 'Taking a chance, aren't you?'

He laughed. 'Both taking a chance, aren't we? This is Strasbourg, not Stratford. . .'

It was half past eight when we got to Heidi Lotl's apartment in the old house of the Boulevard de la Gare off the Place de la Gare. Tall building. François had stopped the truck outside it, that afternoon. We walked up the steps to the fifth floor and arrived at the door of the flat. We'd arranged with François that, if she was at home one of the men I'd met that afternoon would be waiting near the door. The Pole was there. Therefore Heidi was in. If she'd gone out the Pole would have followed her, then reported to François. At the *Deux Elèves*. We'd have gone to the *Deux Elèves*. Second danger; she might have somebody with her. More difficult to check. But we had a way out of that.

David Hinton knocked on the door. I pointed to the bell, and he rang. We waited. After a few minutes, that could have been hours or seconds, the door was opened. On a chain. Though I couldn't see who had opened it, I heard the voice of Heidi Lotl, sounding even richer and fuller now that her bass notes were not cut by the ether.

'Yes? Who is it?' No fear. No suspicion. . .

'We have an urgent message for you.'

'Give it to me.'

'May I ask, Fräulein, if you are alone? The general specified you must be alone when we gave it to you.' She thought for a moment, still out of sight. 'Excuse me,' she said, 'which general?'

Take a chance. It's one in a million. The name of the local commander of the Gestapo was General von Bodendorfer. If she were not alone, if Bodendorfer himself were in there with her. . .

'*Augenblick*,' she said, closed the door, snapped the chain, and opened the door again. She stepped back to let us in, and that gave me a chance to look at her. Dark hair. Dark eyes. Hair straight down the sides of her face and long. Thin nose, small lips, face too long by the merest fraction. Height five feet six inches. Age? Who can tell? Twenty-five? I was twenty-five, Hinton was twenty-seven. She was pretty. Full figure, wearing a dark blue dress in some sort of woollen material. No stockings; probably saved the few pairs she owned for the studio. Pink slippers on her feet, with pink bobbles on the front. Glasses in her hand. Reading, not drinking. She closed the door behind us. Two's safe, she probably thought. She waited patiently for us to give her the message. Hinton coughed, imitating a gentleman's gentleman rather badly. I supposed she assumed he was a high-ranking Gestapo officer in some sort of mufti. She ignored me. Damn strange, he was wearing the same sort of rough worker's clothing I was wearing, but it looked good on him. Mine looked like rag-bags; she thought so too, judging from the smile she beamed on him, and the way she continued to ignore me.

'The general said to make certain you are alone. . .'

She smiled. 'There's no one here,' she said. 'Have a look round, if you must.'

We went together into her sitting-room. It was large and elegantly furnished. The table was covered with papers, and standing on the papers, a wire recorder. The room was about twenty-five feet square and high, at least eleven feet. An elegant room. And warm, at a time when to be warm was a privilege. She must be well protected. Next to the sitting-room was a bedroom, quite small, almost filled by the bed. The clothes cupboards were built into the wall along one side; one of the open doors revealed fitted shelves. The bed, large enough for two people, was unmade. Beside the bed stood a small chest, and on it was a glass containing milky water. The sort you keep false teeth in overnight. She was too young for false teeth, but the flat was warm. I'm not very good at being tidy,' she said, seeing me eye the bed. 'Every so often I become disgusted with myself and leave the apartment for a day or two until someone comes in to clean.'

No one in the kitchen; a packet of fresh-looking pumpernickel. A sausage on a chopping board. A faint odour of real coffee. So she *was* protected. Surprisingly, against the wall, I saw a large professional machine, used for cutting the masters of gramophone records, or the discs from which broadcasts are made. 'Sometimes they send a technician,' she explained, 'and we record here from the next room. We are short of studios and, in an emergency, we use my apartment.'

She had come round with us and was still smiling, though I could tell her patience was beginning to wear thin. Only one other room. For dining or sewing. The table was covered with a velvet cloth, and on the cloth were pins, a hand-operated sewing machine, and a brown paper pattern. We returned to the sitting room.

'Now, please, may I have this mysterious message from General Bodendorfer? You *are* members of his staff . . . you *have* identity cards . . .?'

The air in the apartment was still and warm. Too still, too warm.

From somewhere outside I heard a car, moving slowly along the street, seeking out curfew violators. We were safe inside, and warm. Heidi Lotl looked at us, a warm girl, still smiling. Twenty-five? Five feet six, wearing that dark-blue dress she'd probably made herself, there in the dining-room, spread out on the table. The glasses had not been for reading, but for sewing. Straight home from the studio after her broadcast. Cup of coffee, slice of sausage on pumpernickel. Her breath would smell of garlic, like the sausage did. No general tonight. Quiet evening at home. Making another dress to replace the blue wool. Beautiful eyes, round and set in a long face. Thin nose, small lips. No make-up. Hair long and black but looking soft, not wiry as black hair can be.

'We are British soldiers. My name is Henry Colson. This man's name is David Hinton.' It meant nothing to her. No immediate reaction, that same half-smile, as if she was watching the start of a play, content to let it develop its own drama. Some facts are too big for the mind to grasp at once. 'We're British soldiers. We dropped by parachute, yesterday.'

'Where?'

Does a place name give us credibility? 'Near Wolfisheim.'

'*British* soldiers . . .? Dropped by parachute near Wolfisheim, yesterday?'

'Yes.'

'But why . . .?'

God, she was cool. She sat down, as if interviewing us. She had the detachment of a professional interviewer – 'Oh yes, you've just killed your mother. Would you like to tell us how it happened?'

'I'm listening, Herr Colson.' It almost sounded like, 'I'm waiting'. She looked at me, now ignoring Hinton, but then I guessed she'd always look at the one showing command.

'We need your help.'

'Sabotage?'

I shook my head. It was sabotage, of course, but not the sort she meant. 'No, not sabotage. Herr Hinton is going to make a broadcast on your programme. Tomorrow night he will be your guest of honour.'

'You sound very sure of yourself.'

'I am sure.'

'I already have a guest of honour for tomorrow night. A hospital nurse, back from Africa.'

She sat still. Poised, but always relaxed. 'These interviews are arranged in advance, you must realize. I don't decide. I merely conduct the interview.'

'We thought that was the case. So far as anyone else is concerned, the broadcast tomorrow will take place as usual, but your guest will turn out to be Herr Hinton, and not your nurse from Africa. I presume she has already been recorded?'

'Yes, this afternoon. A good interview.'

'What a pity no one will hear it.'

She stood up, swiftly. I made no attempt to stop her. She came and stood in front of me. 'Look here,' she said, 'I've had enough of this. Who are you? What is this nonsense all about? I have only to pick up the telephone . . .'

So I hit her. Short jab forward with my arm, between her ribs below her breasts. Fist partly clenched, knuckles forward. God, it hurt her. She went backwards off my fist, luckily in line with the chair, and sprawled back into it. I walked forward and bent over her. 'I've come here prepared, if you force me, to kill you. We stay with you, in this apartment, until tomorrow when you'll take us to the broadcasting station and introduce us as friends of yours. We'll go into the studio, and Herr Hinton will make his broadcast. Then we shall leave. But let me tell you this; I'm a soldier, and if anything happens to prevent Herr Hinton making that broadcast, I'll kill you as if you, too, were a soldier. Understand, Miss Lotl. I will KILL YOU, as if you, too, were a soldier.'

Hinton had said nothing, was watching us almost idly.

Her eyes had filled with the tears of pain, but she was not crying. German girls don't cry, eh?

'You animal,' she said.

I reached forward and grabbed her long, black hair. It wasn't wiry, even softer than I had supposed. I pulled her out of the chair and she flinched at first but then stood still near me. I could feel her breathing on my face, and the odour of garlic was not unpleasant. Then I hit her again, the same way, in the same place, let go of her hair and she fell back again into the chair. This time she was in real pain and this time she gagged and started to cry. But then suddenly she bent forwards and was sick over the carpet and my boots.

'Get something from the kitchen,' I said to Hinton, 'and wipe that up.'

He made no protest, went away, came back and cleaned up the mess. I went into the bathroom, took a towel and soaked it, got a glass of water, and came back. She was still bent over, but no longer retching. I pulled back her head, wiped her face with the wet towel, gave her the glass of water. She drank from it, looking at me the whole time and not at Hinton cleaning the carpet. He wiped over my boots and then carried the bowl into the bathroom. I wiped her face again, the tears from her eyes, the perspiration.

'You hurt me,' she said.

I nodded. 'I won't say I'm sorry. But you must understand that I mean what I say. From now on you must do exactly as I tell you. I've no wish to hurt you physically in any way, but I have a job to do, and nothing must prevent it.'

'You *are* an animal . . .' she said. It wasn't an accusation. It wasn't even a condemnation. Merely a statement of fact. I'd descended to the animal level. I'd accepted that I must do something, and, if necessary, was prepared to injure and kill to ensure its success. No appeals to reason. No discussion or argument. Instant obedience with fear of death or physical injury as the only motivation. She reached up and rubbed her chest.

David Hinton had come back from the bathroom and we could hear the lavatory cistern running.

'And you,' she said, 'are you an animal, too? Would *you* like to hit me, to demonstrate that you must win?' She got up out of the chair, walked across the carpet to David Hinton, stood in front of him. 'You too,' she said, 'are you, too, an animal? If so, in God's will, let me know.'

And then she swung her hand wide, and hit him across the cheek. The blow sounded like the crack of a pistol. His face whitened, the red outlines of her fingers coming rapidly through the skin. He looked at me. Then he reached up and placed his hands on each side of her shoulders, holding her arms gently. She glared at him, defying him.

'No,' he said, 'I am not an animal. There is no need to hit me again.'

'You're the one with the soft tongue?' She shrugged off his arms, and went into the bathroom. We let her go. Hinton would have searched it for razors, razor-blades, concealed weapons. I didn't know what to do with my hands; my whole body felt disoriented, as if my arms hung from my shoulders without being connected to me, like the empty sleeves of a disabled soldier's greatcoat.

'I had to let her know we meant business,' I said. He nodded, neither approving nor, for once, disapproving. 'Let's hope she understood. I'd hate to have to kill her,' I said.

When she came from the bathroom her face was red with washing, and her eyes too bright. She looked at David Hinton. 'Herr Hinton,' she said, 'David Hinton *"Stimme aus Berlin"*?'

'Yes, that's me.'

'They said you were dead.

'I was, but now I'm alive again.'

'I used to listen to your broadcasts. You were one of my heroes.'

'I was always nervous.'

'That's part of it, *nicht wahr*?'

'I suppose so.'

'And you, too, parachuted from England?'

'With Herr Colson.'

'Just you, alone . . . ?'

'*Nur du Allein* . . . It's a lovely song . . .'

'Sorry, I didn't mean to ask military secrets.'

'You will cooperate with us?'

She thought for a moment, then sat down again, her hands folded in her lap. 'No, I think not,' she said. 'There are thousands of troops within reach of the broadcasting station. It's in the centre of a large city. As soon as they hear your voice on the air instead of the recorded voice of my nurse from Africa, they'll come to the radio station. Nothing you can do. They'll surround the station; if necessary they'll blow it to the ground. With you and me in it. I don't want to die. Especially not like that. I'd rather die resisting you in any way I can. Somehow I'll find the way. You can't shackle me, you can't injure me, because if you do, you'll never get into the radio station and that's obviously of first importance to you.'

She looked scornfully at me. 'Oh, I realize he's animal enough to kill me – don't worry, you've convinced me of that – but you won't do it until you have no hope. I'll find a way of stopping you. Especially you,' she said, directly at me. 'It's a pity,' she said to David Hinton, 'because I would like to hear your broadcast. From a professional point of view, you understand.' I stood there amazed. She'd taken charge, again, and Hinton didn't know it. I watched her, manipulating him, compelling his interest.

'Shall I tell you something?' she said. 'When I broadcast to the soldiers – you know I do special broadcasts just for the soldiers on a Wednesday evening, and on Wednesdays, I don't wear a brassière, and I don't wear pants. And sometimes when I'm sitting at the microphone, talking to the soldiers, I put my script on the script-stand, and I rub one of my nipples while I'm broadcasting, while I'm speaking, like this, you understand . . .' She leaned forward caressing the outline of her left nipple. David Hinton watched her, transfixed, fascinated. 'Only when I'm talking to the soldiers. I think what I'm doing shows itself in my voice, and I like to think the soldiers feel it.' Hinton was leaning forwards and suddenly she swung the hand she'd been holding by her side forward and upwards. But I'd moved in and my arm shot out; her arm swung against it and she cried with pain as her wrist struck the bony underside of my wrist; her hand opened involuntarily and the small piece of broken mirror came flying into the air; I watched it twirling and when it came down I caught it flat in the palm of my hand. A thin sliver of mascara mirror, a couple of inches long and a half an inch wide at its base; not much, but it could have severed Hinton's jugular, and you can't sew that together. Let him learn the hard way. That'd take the bulge out of his trousers.

She sat back and laughed, rubbing her wrist. 'You see,' she said, 'I played fair. I told you in advance I wouldn't cooperate with you. How many glasses are there in the apartment? Twenty? How many ropes and chains and pieces of mirror and knives and forks and heavy ash-trays and vases and bowls? You don't stand a chance . . .' She laughed again.

'We could tie you.'

'You could, but then you'd have to untie me sometime to get me into the broadcasting station. Incidentally, you know I travel there in a military car? With a driver? You've thought of that. His name is Pieter. He wants me, very badly. Therefore he looks at me all the time. He understands how I'm feeling, all the time. If I'm unhappy, Pieter always knows that. "Not feeling very well today, Fräulein Lotl?" he says. He will immediately know if you are keeping me under restraint. What will you say when he asks me, "not feeling very well today" and I say, so quickly you can't stop me, "these men are keeping me prisoner" . . .?'

Damn, damn. We'd discussed it, the brigadier and I. I didn't want to take Hinton in the first place; I wanted to pre-record him, take the record and play it on the air. It would have been a lot easier. But the brigadier had asked what I would do if the record suddenly developed a repeating groove. Records do that. For no apparent reason. 'And now, listeners, we have David Hinton to talk to you . . .' and he came on with a repeat. They'd laugh us out of Germany.

If we'd taken a record, I wouldn't have needed Heidi Lotl. I could have smashed my way into the broadcasting station and taken over the apparatus and broadcast anything I damned well pleased. But finally, I had to agree with the brigadier that the value in the exercise lay in its normality; if Heidi made a 'normal' broadcast, and her guest was a real, live David Hinton. 'You'll be obliged to strike her, just to convince her you mean business, but you'll have no more trouble.' I'd even asked the quack. If you want to hit somebody, not kill them, not bruise them anywhere it will show, but really hurt them, where would you do it? And we'd stood before a drawing of the human body and discussed it. The kidneys? Very painful, but it can do an injury, can incapacitate a person.

Only after rejecting several possibilities had we decided on the place I'd hit her, in the centre of the body, between the curve of the ribs. But not with the palm of my hand. That could have broken her ribs, could have killed her. Damn it, we'd agreed that once I'd persuaded her I had the brutality to kill her, she'd be docile and we'd only need to watch her carefully. But this girl was made of tougher stuff than we'd anticipated. I didn't want to hit her again. It would be an empty gesture. I didn't want her eyes following me around the apartment all night if we tied her up.

'Would you care for some coffee?' she asked me. 'Perhaps a slice of wurst? I have fresh pumpernickel, and I can tell from the way you speak German you must be used to German food. You must have lived here at some time. I even have a little wine. No schnapps, alas.'

I didn't respond.

'I know,' she said. 'There's a girl who works at the station. Very pretty. I'm sure you'll like her . . . why don't I give her a ring, ask her to come round, and we can have supper together, and a bit of a party. You'll both like her . . .'

'For Christ's sake, shut up . . .'

Brief flash of fear in her eyes as I took a half step towards her; a quick thought that perhaps she'd gone too far. Hinton laughed. He'd placed himself neatly outside my dilemma. 'It's all yours,' his laugh seemed to say. I rounded on him. 'You shut up, too, and go and make yourself useful in the kitchen . . .'

'Coffee and pumpernickel, sir?'

'No. Tea and M&V.'

'We thought you'd be short, so we've brought our own food,' he said to Heidi as he fished in his suitcase. He took out a tin of tea/sugar/milk powder, M&V stew, barley-sugars, hard-tack biscuits and what they said was potato in powder form. I didn't believe them. Then he brought out the unauthorized items. The crafty sod. I cursed myself; I ought to have thought of that. He put the items on the table beside her and she picked them up, one by one. A bar of Pears Golden Glory soap. Two toothbrushes. Two, when the NAAFI allowance was one every six months if you were lucky. A roll of toilet paper. Not the smooth, hard Army issue, but civilian, soft, from Timothy White's and Taylors. A lipstick. A box of sanitary napkins, a vanity mirror. 'Somehow, I don't think you'd better have that,' he said, slipping it into his inside pocket. 'At least, not just yet.' A tin of peaches, more barley-sugars, but these in a flat tin with a civilian label on it. And a bottle of Camp Coffee Essence. The real stuff.

'You're married?' she said to him.

'Good Lord, no,' he said. 'I asked a married lady to put me up a parcel for you. She wanted to go to Fortnum and Mason's, but I didn't think that was on.' He went into the kitchen. She looked at her presents.

'I feel like a Red Indian,' she said, laughing gently. 'Thank God you didn't bring me any beads.'

'Or a tomahawk, made in Birmingham...'

'Birmingham, where is that...?'

'It doesn't matter.'

'Oh, but it *does* matter. If you're going to stay with me until tomorrow's broadcast, we must find a subject of conversation. You must tell me about England. What is Fortnum and Mason? What is Birmingham?'

Damn the brigadier. Damn Hinton. Damn Heidi. Damn all women who don't behave as they should do. By rights she should have been scared witless. Cowering in her chair saying 'don't hit me again'. Crying. I'm *only* a woman. Please take pity on me. Hinton was whistling in the kitchen, making supper. She was sitting relaxed in her chair, smiling at me. *Um Gottes Will.* We couldn't walk out of that door with her tomorrow, in her present mood. She'd tell the first person we met. Two Englanders. *Fallschirmjaegers.* And die smiling. Death's the ultimate fear, and she wasn't afraid of it. At twenty-five.

'Who wears the false teeth?'

'False teeth . . .?'

'The glass, beside the bed.'

'Ah, the false teeth. I have a comrade . . .'

'What is he, some doddering old general? Perhaps Bodendorfer?'

She laughed again. 'If you must know, he was a pilot in the Luftwaffe, until you shot away his undercarriage and he had to crash. He broke all his front teeth. He crashlanded a Messerschmitt and all he broke was his teeth. Now he wears false ones. They don't affect the way he looks. If anything, he looks even more handsome with them, so white and even. He's thirty years old. Taller than you are. More handsome than you are. And a good lover, which I bet you are not. Though I don't want to find out. He has a beautiful body; a true *Valhalla* body. He makes me so satisfied, sexually.'

'Then why mess about rubbing your nipples?'

'I made that up. For your friend. He has hot eyes, that one.'

'I'll tell him.'

'No, you won't. You don't like him, do you? Your friend. He doesn't like you. I don't think you're the same kind of man, are you? You both speak excellent German, but you learned yours in the bars. He learned his in the salons. He's like my friend. Didn't I tell you? A von Rosenheiler. Descended from a cousin of the late Kaiser. Something you so obviously are not, and your friend Herr Hinton so obviously is; an aristocrat.'

'He still makes lousy tea,' I said, looking at the flyspecks floating on the cup of liquid Hinton had placed before me. A tray, with a cloth; meat and vegetable stew on a plate, with a saucepan lid on it as if it were a silver cover to the country house kidneys; tea in cups, with saucers. Salt, pepper and, crowning touch, to complete the humbling process, a napkin.

'This belongs to von Rosenheiler, no doubt?' I said to Heidi.

'No. I think his batman left it here, but please, do use it. I can always wash it afterwards.'

Heidi and Hinton took their meal at the table. I remained seated where I was, eating mine off the tray.

'Did he say von Rosenheiler?' Hinton asked.

She nodded. At least she wasn't too proud to eat the food we'd brought.

'Willie von Rosenheiler?'

'No, Freddie. Willie's cousin. Did you know him? Before the war? At Freinigen?'

'I never went to Freinigen,' Hinton said. 'We hunted in Poland.'

'Freinigen was great fun. You should have come. The dances, the food . . .'

'I hear the sailing was good . . .?'

'If you like it. I never did. So, you know Willie von Rosenheiler. Wait until I tell Freddie. He'll be sorry to have missed you. . .'

'That at least is good news,' I said. Both of them turned towards me as if suddenly remembering my presence. 'That he'll miss us.'

'He's in Friedrichshafen for five days. He went three days ago.'

Old folks week. A bloody reunion.

'Hinton,' I said, 'get off your bloody arse and wash these plates.'

I looked at my watch. Half past ten. Time was flying by; it seemed we'd only been there ten minutes instead of an hour and a half. 'You,' I said to Heidi, 'get off to bed.' Let her lie there, thinking about what *could* happen to her if she didn't do what I had asked.

'I usually bathe first . . .'

'Then be quick about it . . .'

She came to stand by the chair on which I was sitting. 'Where are you going to sleep?' she asked.

74

'I'm not . . . I shall be watching you, every second.'

'Until Herr Hinton goes to sleep . . .?'

'And then?'

'I can't see you missing a chance like this. To crawl into bed with me. Or are you queer?'

'You can't provoke me, you know. What have you palmed? A knife off the table? The pepper-pot? Rubbing your chest may work with Hinton, but it leaves me cold.'

'Are you afraid of women?'

'I left a girl behind who makes you seem like a nun . . .' I stood up, feeling inferior with her standing over me. The NAAFI girl would have been thrilled by my comparison. She couldn't hold a candle to Heidi Lotl.

'If you're prepared to kill me, you wouldn't baulk at a rape,' she said, taunting me. I placed my hand on her breast, looked into her eyes. 'You're an attractive woman and I don't doubt you're marvellous in bed. But believe me, all I can feel at this moment is a woollen dress. Nothing more. A woollen dress, with a bulge in it.'

She pouted. 'I'll take a bath,' she said, 'and then we'll see.'

My hand rode along her shoulder and I grasped the top of her arm and swung her round. Chop, at her wrist. Hand open, uncontrolled. Chop again, other hand open. Nothing in either hand; no slivers of glass, no knives, no pepper-pots. When I let go, she laughed.

'Never know, will you? Fifteen hours together. I'll take a bath and climb into a large warm bed. I usually wear a short nightgown, but not even that tonight.'

I turned her, put my arms around her and dragged her to me. Held her tight, looking at her face so close to me. Her lips were moist. She parted them, and the tip of her tongue licked them, side to side. 'You've got the strength in those arms,' she whispered, 'to hit me, to kill me, to do anything you like with me.'

I kissed her and her arms went about me and she held me to her. Her lips rubbed beneath mine and her body pressed close to me. I brought my hands round and lightly touched the ends of my thumbs on her nipples, beneath that woollen

75

dress. She turned slightly to the side, and her knees parted and she held my leg between her thighs. I could feel the hardness of the bone and she rubbed against me, knowing I had lied about the dress, knowing that already she was beginning to excite me. 'You've got the strength,' she said when our lips parted, 'why don't you use it on me?'

It would have been so easy to say her hunger was as great as mine; it would have been easy to let myself be washed along by that great wave of passion. I held her breasts now, and they moved beneath my hands, and her thighs were clamped around my leg, pulsing, throbbing, pleading.

I had enough juice in me to spend the entire time until we went to the studio on that bed with her and even then I knew that neither one of us would be satisfied. She reached down her hand and touched me. 'You want me,' she said, and started to kiss me again.

I knew that dangerous moment of sexuality when every thought, every instinct, every responsibility, is subordinated to that one consuming desire, to thrust flesh into flesh, to enter, to take, and then to combine. My hands reached down to her buttocks and I pulled her hard into me, feeling the thrust of her Venus mound against me.

'Yes, I want you,' I said, lifting my lips a millimetre from hers, feeling her warm, moist breath on my mouth. I was erect and ground the hardness of it into her and she knew she could make me harder still, and take me inside herself, and drain me dry. And conquer me. But I pulled away from her, and drew back my head so that I could look into her eyes. She ought to have kissed me then, but she didn't. She ought to have held me tight, but she didn't. She ought to have lifted her dress and pulled me down to the carpet and scrabbled at my clothing until she had exposed me, and taken me, and locked me hard and firm inside herself. But she didn't.

'Go and have your bath,' I said to her, 'and then I'll tuck you up in bed and I'll read you a bedtime story, about a big, bad wolf who tried to eat a sweet little piggie and wound up in a pot of boiling water . . .'

CHAPTER SIX

When Sergeant-Major Dai Williams came down the hill at 22.00.00 on the night before the broadcast, François was waiting for him with the truck and the squad. The sergeant-major, Freddie and Frank, John and Jack and Jim all climbed aboard, took the long-handled shovels.

'We have to wait,' François said. 'Five minutes.' The truck had been pulled into a small track beneath trees. It was invisible from the road. The Dutchman, Henk, was standing in the trees by the roadside. Several German military vehicles went past but saw nothing. Bright night, but no moon.

'Everything going according to plan?' Dai Williams asked François. He was a man used to routine, carrying out the orders of his superiors, which he accepted without question. He'd been born and bred up in the Brecon Beacons and, though the industrial towns of the Ebbw Vale were near, he had never had sufficient interest to go down the hillside to them. His father owned a small cottage in the middle of a thousand acres of common land. Sheep grazed there, and Welsh mountain ponies; the ground was covered with peat and moss, bracken and ferns, gorse and wild flowers. In that natural setting Dai Williams had flourished. He was a strangely silent boy whose only interest seemed to be the out-of-doors; who wouldn't read a book but would spend hours with a scrap of paper and a pencil drawing rock formations, details of flowers or animals. His father had no objections; Dai fed the pot regularly with rabbits and hares, even partridge and pheasant. He could find a lost sheep by instinct and knew the mountain flocks so well that frequently he was called in to settle a dispute of ownership. When the war came, he walked down into Ebbw Vale. He was twenty-one and they took him immediately for the South Wales Borderers. His first instructors were amazed; he could fire a rifle better than any of them; strip a gun down he'd never seen before and reassemble it faster than anyone they'd ever watched. When they came to teach him fieldcraft, he was confused at first since he could not relate the ground, directions and distances, to map and compass, but let him put aside these unnatural aids and he could walk straight as an arrow along any direction they showed him, cross any field unseen, light a fire even in the pouring rain. When they were forming the first Special Services without having much of an idea what the 'Specials' would have to do, they tapped him as an instructor. He'd been instructing a year when they sent him on his first job. Since then, he'd never cared to go back to school, not even as a teacher. Let Dai Williams loose on a piece of ground and it became an open book; he could look at a field of grass, observe the way the blades of grass were bent and tell you immediately what animals, including human, had used it; listen to the birds cawing hundreds of yards away and say if they had been frightened by a cat or a human.

Through no fault of his own, his first job with Special Services was a disaster, and the eight men who'd been put ashore with him near Calais were all captured. Dai escaped the Germans by hiding immobile in a wood for three days and nights. When he came out he went for food to a remote farmhouse, and while he was eating there, the Germans came and occupied the farm as a military outpost. Dai hid in the roof for four months, with the farmer as his sole companion for an hour each evening. The roof was never searched. During that time the farmer, who had come back from Provence in 1937 to take over his father's holding, taught Dai to speak French. Dai tried to teach the farmer English in exchange, but the farmer was past learning, or perhaps too scared he would blurt out a wrong word among the Germans.

When, after a season, the outpost was abadoned, the farm returned to war-time normality, and Dai was helped to escape down The Line by the local *Maquis*. He got back to England five weeks later, having added fluent French to his other qualifications. As soon as the MO pronounced him fit again he re-volunteered for Special Services.

Dai stood in the back of the open truck, waiting, senses alert. He glanced at his watch, saw the sweep second-hand come round. 'They're early,' he said.

No one else had heard the distant crack of the charges, but within a second they all saw the start of the pyrotechnic display of red splashes of fire against the evening sky. One explosion down the road, away from Strasbourg; several to the left, in Strasbourg itself. And then they heard the slow rumble of the explosions that had caused the soaring tongues of flame, the plumes of white smoke.

'That'll keep 'em busy,' François said, then banged the roof of the cab. The driver started the engine and drove out of the lane, left to Strasbourg. At the bottom of the lane Henk, despite his wooden leg, swung aboard. 'Nothing doing on the road,' he said, 'but there soon will be. Did you see the flare when Poincarre's stack went up? That was one of mine...'

The explosions and the flares were designed to be nothing more than a nuisance, a hay-rick burning, a dump of waste near the town, a disused shop. But under cover of the explosion and the flames, the lorry of the Ministry of Public Works could move about freely, even during the hours of the curfew.

The surroundings of the Parc des Ouvriers were deserted; the lorry stopped near the fence and the Englishmen jumped off. Inside the fence were shrubs and trees which hid them from view of the houses. Three hundred yards away, at the corner of the fence where it bent sharply to the right, the German guard post. Four men and a sergeant. The fence was closed at that point by large, iron gates, ten feet high, twelve feet wide. Anyone going into the park to the broadcasting station had to pass through a wicker door set next to the gate and walk between railings under bright illumination past the window and the door of the guard-house itself. Only people with passes were allowed in since the evening transmissions started at 6 PM.

Freddie and Frank immediately got to work on the wire

while the driver took the lorry round into a side street and parked it, with the Frenchman sitting down in the back. The wire was ten feet high, diamond mesh on four straining wires of tensile steel. The straining wires were connected to spring-loaded alarms every hundred metres; no attempt was made to cut them. As each link of the diamond mesh was cut, Frank slipped the two cut ends into steel clip tubes he'd brought with him. They cut out a panel four feet high by about three feet wide; but clipped into position, you couldn't see it had been severed. One extra strong push, however, and that panel would spring open like a door.

Next stop Rue de la Principalité, one of the eight roads that led to the Parc des Ouvriers. This time the lorry drove quite openly, and parked over a manhole in the road. The workmen quickly erected a barrier round the lorry, and John and Jack went down the manhole, into the electric conduit. It was about a metre square, two metres deep, and running out of it across the street, a conduit box carried electric mains wires. John and Jack worked quickly, preparing the explosives with detonators and fuse cords, poking them along the conduit as far as they could get them.

While they were working they heard a motor-bike patrol stop in the street above them, but ignored it. François talked to the patrol, showed them his Ministry of Public Works authority, agreed with them that these 'damned sabotage bombs going off all over the city were a nuisance', and they drove off.

Next stop the Rue Honoré de Balzac, again leading to the park. The lorry parked by an abandoned building. The workmen erected a barrier round a manhole, but Freddie and Frank went into the deserted building. This time they planted their explosives against the front wall; when that was blown, the whole building would fall down into the street, blocking it completely.

Each road leading to the park was mined. A tank could get through the blocks without too much difficulty; but the nearest tanks were twenty minutes away. A lorry could get to the block carrying men, but on foot it would take the men ten minutes at least to get to the Parc entrances, another six or seven to come near the broadcasting station, deep inside the Parc.

The squad climbed through the gap in the wire and clipped it shut behind them. It would stand daytime inspection. They kept close to the fence in the shrubberies, banked azaleas, and rhododendrons, with which this side of the Parc was lined. In the middle of the shrubberies, out of sight of the main walks of the Parc, was a hut in which grass-cutting equipment was stored in the winter. It took Jim only a minute to pick the padlock; it was a damned sight warmer in there than on the hill-top, and they could boil tea and heat M&V. Even smokeless fuel tablets give off the light of a flame. The sergeant-major and Jim took the first watch; Jim inside the hut, the sergeant-major comfortably concealed in the shrubberies.

He felt more at home with the stars above his head, the sound of the water of the River Ill in his ears. Slowly he identified the noises in the shrubberies; several cats, birds squeaking in fear and annoyance, field-mice, rats. It had all gone very well, he thought. He'd worried when Major Castleford had to drop out, but Captain Colson was a man who knew his onions.

Footsteps along the path. To be expected. They patrol the path. A squirrel ran, chattering a warning. Regular stampede through the shrubberies as they all scarper from the footsteps. Regular rhythm. Rustle of cloth on cloth as whoever it is walks along. Clink of his rifle on his belt, or the buckle of it. Poor bugger. Bet he's scared bloody silly, walking round the park in the dark. Jump out at him and shout 'boo' and he'd shit himself. Regular townie, probably. A country lad would walk along the edge of the grass, making less sound. But a townie probably needs the sound of his own footsteps to reassure himself.

Regular rhythm. Twenty yards away, fifteen, ten. That's as near as he comes. Footsteps stop. Oh yes, he's going to have a smoke, or a piss. He can't have seen anything. Nothing to see; we came in at the back of the shrubberies. Nothing to hear; the sergeant-major hadn't moved an inch, hadn't exhaled a breath. Jesus Christ in Heaven! What if this bastard uses the hut for a quick kip and a smoke while he's supposed to be touring the perimeter of the Parc? That must be it. Into the hut, quick drink from a bottle he's hidden there, maybe a smoke. Dai Williams rose slowly in the midst of the shrub. Dark beyond the shrub, but not so dark the sergeant-major couldn't see the track that led from the main path to the hut. He turned slightly, moving in complete silence, feet apart, hands held out at his sides. If he comes down the path . . . If he comes. Let him pass, then chop him behind the ear. Then what? They have to find him. Natural accident. Hit him with a branch from a tree and leave the branch beside the body. They'll think a branch fell from a tree. But they don't, do they. Dead branches don't fall from trees with enough force to kill anyone wearing a steel hat. All right, take off his steel hat and loop it round his wrist, so they'll think he took it off to get some fresh air to his head; and then hit him on the top of the head with a dead branch that *could* have killed him, if it had dropped from a tree. They won't go to all the bother of climbing a tree to see where the branch came from, will they? Very unlikely. No sound. The man was still. Not pissing, the sergeant-major would have heard that. Not doing anything. Standing perfectly still, in the dark, ten yards away. What's he doing?

Whatever it was, Dai would never know. The regular beat of footsteps started again, as the man resumed his solitary night patrol of the Parc. Without turning his head he spoke softly. 'Okay, he's gone.'

The figure of Jim materialized beside him. 'How did you know it was me?' he said. The sergeant-major chuckled.

'I heard you open the door a bit wider, when I got up. And then I heard you walking down the path towards me. . .'

'If I'd been a German . . .'

'You'd have been dead, lad! This isn't a tin-opener I've got in my hand. . .'

Jim turned to go back into the hut. 'By the way, lad,' the sergeant-major said, 'thanks for keeping an eye on me. Many-a-one would have dropped off, in the warm.'

'Don't thank me, Sergeant-Major, thank that bloody M&V. I think it must have been tinned for the Boer War and I've had the trots ever since I ate it.'

CHAPTER SEVEN

Heidi, not asleep, was sitting up in bed, without her nightie, as she had threatened. She dragged the bed across the room before she got into it, and opened the door so that I could see her. Now she was sitting there, and I'd left the light on. Naked and unashamed. Still hopeful? Her breasts were firm, her nipples small and dark red against the pink of the ring that surrounded them. The palms of my hands tingled at the memory. Why not climb into bed with her? Why not dominate her that way, too? For one thing, it'd be a damned sight more exciting than spending the night fighting sleep, sitting in the chair watching her. Why not take her, on her terms? And enjoy myself, on my terms. It would be yet another challenge, wouldn't it? Could I get into that bed, and enjoy her, and not for one second lose control of the situation? She was hoping to get me to drop my guard, to bring me to that state of euphoria which follows sex. And then, the bitch would kill me, without compunction. I'd had enough challenges for one day.

Hinton had gone to sleep; cool bastard. He'd stretched himself out along her horse-hair sofa, wrapped himself in one of her spare blankets, and had gone to sleep. Just like that. Cheeky bastard. 'Cup of tea, Henry, about seven?'

'Yes, your worship, and shall I draw a bath . . .?'

Dark in the street outside. Very little transport moving about, now that the excitement of the explosions at ten o'clock had died down. I'd been looking at my watch, waiting for them. This damned watch gained, and I'd had to subtract a few seconds, but the explosions seemed to have happened on time. For a while lorries had rushed along the street, fire engines clanging, motor bikes revving wildly. Perfect cover for Dai, François, and the boys. Good thinking on the part of the brigadier; if you can't hide them, give them a reason for being there.

Hinton moved in his sleep. Restless. Dreaming of pheasant and port?

Earlier when I had told her to go to bed, she went into the bathroom, drew a bath, used the lavatory. I heard the cistern running. Scrubbed her teeth; I heard the brush going. The new NAAFI brush Hinton had brought. Then she got into the bath with Hinton's soap; I heard her sigh luxuriously. Hot water; this must be a special apartment, with a boiler that was kept working despite the fuel shortage. Ex-Luftwaffe pilots don't pull that much rank. So who was her protector? Would he appear, later that night, to collect the rent in bed? Back to the window, slip behind the blackout curtain. Nothing moved in the street below, nor along the main street I could see at the end of it.

'Captain,' she said, 'stop prowling about.'

Captain? How the hell did she know that? Had Hinton used my rank?

I went into her bedroom. Still sitting up in bed. No attempt to hide her breasts. They were firm and high, and . . . stop that! They were a pair of tits – nothing more, nothing less.

'How did you know I am a Captain?'

She looked me in the eyes, smiling. Damn it, woman, you should be cowering back in the bed, bundled up in the bed clothes, saying 'don't hurt me'.

'Obvious. They don't send Lieutenants on missions such as this one. You can't have much higher rank, or Herr Hinton would show at least some signs of respect. Will you really make him tea in the morning, before you waken him?'

'All right, if you're so smart, Fräulein, what rank does your Herr Hinton hold, your aristocratic Herr Hinton?'

She thought for a moment, looking out into the other room, though she couldn't see Hinton on the sofa from the bed. 'Somehow, I don't think it would matter to him what rank he held. He could either be a – how do you call it, a general? – or even a private soldier. To him, that would not have any importance.'

She was right, of course; he already had all the rank he could use in civilian life, the ultimate accolade of 'gentlemen'.

'But *you* care for such things, don't you?' she persisted.

I shook my head, went out of the bedroom to the window, checked the street outside again, went to the door of the apartment, opened it a crack, listened in the hallway.

'Do stop pacing about,' she said, when I came back in. Hinton was still fast asleep. I had a perverse desire to waken him. She chuckled softly and I went back into her bedroom and sat on the chair beside her bed. What was I afraid of, dammit? Sweat on my upper lip. Okay, face it, and conquer it. Her breasts were exciting me. The thought of her naked body in that bed was exciting me. I wanted the sexual experience of her, there and then, in that bed. Okay, so that meant I was normal. Nothing queer about me; see a pair of tits and want to stroke 'em, nothing wrong in that.

But I knew quite clearly those 'tits' meant failure of the mission to me, and possibly even death.

We were looking at each other. 'All right,' she said. 'You win ...'

It was a temporary victory.

She surprised me when she spoke again. 'Do you believe the Allies will win the war?' she asked.

'Do you believe the Germans will win?'

'If you mean the fight against the Allies ... Yes. I believe that one day we'll have a German in Buckingham Palace. A German House of Commons ... Yes.'

'Where's your sense of history? Nationality is an ephemeral thing anyway. Queen Victoria filled the Royal House of Europe with her progeny; some of our Members of Parliament can't speak the English language properly ...'

'If, on the other hand,' continued Heidi, as if I hadn't spoken, 'you mean, "will we win the war against ourselves?" that's a different question. If Kaiser William had not made such a fool of himself, acting a part in the years before the last war ...'

'If an Archduke had not died at Sarajevo, and Rasputin had died in Russia . . .'

'You are laughing at me,' she said, pouting again. But then she became more serious, and hunched herself across the bed, drawing nearer to me. I reached out and opened one of her hands where it lay on the counterpane. Then the other hand. Neither contained a sliver of glass.

'I don't want to be killed,' she said. 'I'm just a very ordinary person. I'm not one of these fanatical people who believe you should be prepared to give your life for what you believe. I could never kill someone, just for a belief. I could defend myself; I think I could even kill someone to defend myself. I wouldn't have slashed Herr Hinton with that glass, you know. I don't want to be killed, not even for Germany.'

'I don't take any delight in killing, not even Germans.'

'But you're prepared to kill me.'

'If I have to . . .'

'Who decides . . . ?'

'I do. It's a question of priorities. Hinton must make that broadcast, and we need you to get into the broadcasting station without fuss.'

'If I promise to do that . . . ?'

'I promise not to kill you . . .'

'So simple?'

'Yes, so simple. Look. I have nothing against you personally. It's just rotten luck, so far as you are concerned, that you happen to be the woman who makes those broadcasts.'

'But it is *me*. I *am* the woman who makes the broadcasts . . .'

'Then make it. We don't care about that. So long as Hinton makes it with you . . .'

'But I can't see how that will help you. The minute he finishes speaking, I'll go back on the air, provided you don't kill me, and explain exactly who he is and how he comes to be making such a broadcast. I shall urge them to ignore everything he's said. And they listen to me. If they didn't listen to me, I wouldn't have a national programme . . .'

'And we wouldn't be here, eh?'

86

Now she had put her hand in mine, was grasping my hand as if to emphasize her point. I ached to put my other arm around her slim, naked shoulder; to draw her to me, to comfort her. Phoney. We both knew what I wanted.

'I don't know if I can explain this to you,' I said, 'but you've got a Germanic approach. You think in absolutes, black and white. Anyone not in active support of the Third Reich is actively against the Third Reich. We allow for differences of degree. All right. Hinton makes his broadcast. You come on afterwards and contradict him. But millions of people will have listened to him, and some will ask themselves, is what he says true? Can it be true? He spreads the seeds of doubt. Your people haven't been given any room for doubt. The Third Reich is the sum total of all glory, and anything else must be crushed and ruthlessly destroyed. The world consists of Aryans and The Rest, and The Rest must be annihilated. Hinton will spread seeds of doubt. Just a few. Perhaps those seeds won't grow, perhaps they will. It's not my responsibility to assess that.'

'But you accept your responsibility to kill me . . .?'

'If necessary.'

She gripped my hand. 'I don't want to be killed,' she said, looking into my eyes, as if seeking some spark of warmth, some trace of compassion.

'Then you must help us. It's quite simple. All you have to do, is to do nothing, other than what I tell you. It won't last long, and when we have gone, you can say anything you like, on the air or off it. You needn't be afraid. The Gestapo will interrogate you, of course. They'll ask you over and over and over again why you didn't try to escape, or warn somebody. If it will help you, I'll even let Hinton spill a little of his blood over your carpet, so that you can prove you put up a struggle. After all, it is true. You did try to resist.'

'I never thought you'd fall for it. . .'

'But you could have slashed his vein if I hadn't stopped you. You could have killed him. Can you complain if the same thing happens to you? Especially since, if it does happen, it'll be your own fault. . .'

'That's the trouble. It won't be my own fault. I just can't

help myself. Oh, I'm not one of your fanatical Rhine-maidens. I long ago ceased to believe in the Glory of the Third Reich. The army consists of ordinary men and women, just like you and me. The men manipulating them in most cases don't believe in Hitler. *Der Fuehrer* is an idea, not a man. We have our share of good men and evil, just as any other country does. But, like all other countries, we believe our cause is right, our cause is just. We must fight you, don't you understand, for no more reason than that we are Germans. I – am – a – German.' Each word was punctuated vehemently, and perhaps the sound of her vehemence pierced David Hinton's subconscious, for he stirred in his sleep and moaned slightly. I couldn't understand what she was saying. My passport called me British but I couldn't see myself fighting and killing just because I *was* British. No one was more British than Hinton, and yet Hinton had broadcast for the *Germans*, a traitor to the British. Dai Williams was Welsh, living in a conquered country.

'You must understand,' she said. 'I will have to try to resist you, for no more reason than that I am a German, and you are British. And for this, you are going to kill me.'

Unaccountably, I remembered my first girl. The actual words I'd used. It was after a village dance, and I'd taken her into a cowshed, on the straw. I didn't rape her – at least, I don't consider I raped her. She put up a token resistance but it was the sort of thing I expected. A girl must preserve her reputation. 'We mustn't,' she said, 'you mustn't.' And kept on saying it, even after I had entered her. And all I could think of to say was – 'I've got to . . . I must . . .' and when she asked me why, I said, 'Because I'm a man and you're a woman.' That wasn't even true; I was a boy and she was a girl, and we were both human beings, not animals. Afterwards, I was disgusted with myself.

Heidi lifted my hand and placed it on her breast. 'And all you felt was a woollen dress?' she asked. My hand cupped her breast, and her hand fell away. I was free to take my hand away, but I didn't. She moved her head closer to mine, and I was free to kiss her, but I didn't. She slid slowly down in the bed so that I had to bend over her to keep my hand on her breast. It was firm and warm, and I could feel her nipple slowly coming to life under my hand, without even realizing that my hand had slowly started its own erotic rotation. 'I don't want you to kill me,' she said. 'I want you to make love to me.'

She brought up her hands and placed them around my body, pulling me gently on to the bed, drawing my face nearer to hers. I was hypnotized by the sight of her moist lips, her bright eyes, the pulse of her breast in my hand.

'It isn't like it was before. I don't want to kill you. But I really do want you to make love to me ...'

'So that *I* can't kill *you* ...?'

'I don't believe you could. If you wanted to convince me what an animal you've become, you'd have raped me, or at least you'd have taken me there, in the other room when we both wanted to. But you didn't. You struck me, but I saw the shame in your eyes when you did it. After you'd done it I felt your remorse.'

And then she kissed me. This time, the kiss was genuine, not provocative. This time the kiss was sincere. For a brief moment I tasted toothpaste, and then that was gone. I can't describe the yearning that kiss gave me, the desire to be somewhere else with her, at some other time. The longing to be normal, male and female, in some other surroundings. Her lips were moist and rich and full and she rubbed them gently against my lips, and my hand tightened gently on her breast as if all my longings were flowing through my fingertips. The kiss was a kiss of forgetfulness; it erased the past, the future, left only the warm commanding present.

'There'll be no glass,' she said when our lips came apart. 'I promise. The rest of the night. Just you and me. Let's forget the war, being German and British, Hinton, the broadcast, everything. The rest of the night, just you and me.'

CHAPTER EIGHT

It was shortly after four o'clock in the morning when Henk turned up for work. By arrangement. Klaus was waiting for him. 'How did it go?' Klaus asked him.

'Very well. I'm grateful to you.'

'Any time. I can use the money.'

'*Heil Hitler.*'

'*Heil Hitler.* See you at eight this evening.'

'Yes, see you.'

Klaus took out his curfew pass and placed it ready in the pocket of his overcoat. Telephone exchange workers were classified 'essential' and given night passes. Klaus was always glad to help a pal, especially when the pal not only swapped duties but also paid for the privilege. Klaus was not going straight home to his wife. Not likely, with Henk's money burning a hole in his pocket. The Officers' brothel on the Avenue des Cloches was open all night.

Henk checked along the bays. Nothing to see; nothing urgent to do. He went into the switchboard room; two men and four girls bright as buttons. They went off duty at nine o'clock, so he was in no hurry.

You can disable a telephone switchboard in a number of ways. You can deprive it of electric power by cutting the main current line, but switchboards are connected to emergency power supplies, and those need to be cut, too. You can blow up the selectors, and then nothing works; you can cut all the incoming cables. Or, you can do as Henk did; you can arrange to cut off the part of the apparatus that connects to the ringing tone; then, even though a subscriber gets a dialling tone, dials normally, and can hear the other telephone apparently ringing, the distant telephone bell never rings, so the receiver never knows someone is trying to call him. The result, we hoped, would be chaos.

We wanted the Gestapo to waste time, picking up their

telephones and dialling, listening to the ringing tone at the far end and waiting, waiting, waiting.

It took Henk about three hours to do the preliminary wiring. Now, by pressing a switch he'd installed in the Central Processing Unit, the CPU, he could cripple the entire Strasbourg telephone system.

The damage wouldn't be either apparent, or permanent. As soon as he'd finished, he could disconnect the switch and his wiring, and no one would know it had been there. After all, he didn't want to lose his job . . . He went into the switchboard room. The SS man was sitting at his table, trying to look fierce, giving an imitation of a watch dog, not very successfully. Anne was sitting at her 'desk' and beckoning Henk over. 'This cord of mine,' she said, 'it's getting all frayed. I told Klaus, but you know what he is, too busy messing about in the switch-room there.'

'I'll change it for you,' Henk said, 'while you're having your coffee.' He looked down the bank of desks. 'I think all these cords could do with changing. I'll fix the lot, one at a time, while you each take a breakfast break. All right, Adolf?' he asked the SS man.

The SS man came and looked at the frayed cord of the girl's headset. 'It looks all right to me,' he said. 'We have to be economic. Why not bind the thing round with a piece of tape?'

'How would you like it, if we bound your thing round with a piece of tape?' Anne said, cheekily. He'd pushed his headset down onto his shoulders and the cord dangled by his side. He held it up and showed it to them.

'Mine's in good order,' he said.

'I wasn't talking about that one,' Anne said, as she slipped out of her headset and went to the staff canteen.

Once again they'd caught him! The SS man flushed with anger. 'And Adolf is not my name,' he said to Henk. 'How many times must I tell you?'

Henk didn't listen. He'd already swung out the panel of the 'desk', and was unwinding the cord through its clips. Adolf stumped away, back to his post, plugged himself in, and switched in to one of the conversations. One of these days, he'd show the lot of them. Henk glanced at him. Adolf wasn't watching. Now comes the tricky bit. He had to disable the coil activators, so that, when a call came through, it wouldn't show up on the board. One by one, he had to go along the 'desks' doing the same thing. It had to be done in such a way that he could activate it when he wished, and deactivate it so that no one would know if they examined the desk. The SS men were all trained switchboard operators and mechanics. They would know at a glance what was wrong, if they saw him doing it. It was quite a wiring feat, and it would take him all day to do it. Thank God Klaus had given him the extra time by innocently swapping part of his duty with Henk.

When Anne came back from breakfast, she had a new, clean cord on her headset. 'That's worth a kiss,' she said, and lightly pecked Henk on his cheek. The extra wire that led to the extra switch was out of sight behind her desk. She wouldn't have known what it was if she'd seen it. A light had come on. She plugged in a jack, sat down, drew a pad towards herself, held her pencil ready and with it, pushed forward the 'speak' key. 'Strasbourg Central,' she said, 'can I help you?'

Henk was already working on Melanie's 'desk'. He selected a blue cord for her. To match her eyes.

CHAPTER NINE

They were all awake in the hut in the Parc des Ouvriers.

'That bloody M&V,' Jim said, for the hundredth time. They all groaned in sympathy. They all had the trots. 'My arsehole feels as if it's on fire,' John said, sitting up clutching his stomach, his sleeping bag wrapped round his legs ready to pull off. Jim looked round the hut in the half-light; they looked a miserable crew, all clutching their guts. 'Go out and see the sergeant-major,' Freddie said, 'and ask him to come in here.'

Jim went cautiously through the door, hit the deck despite the pain in his guts, and squirmed his way forward through the shrubberies. One minute he was alone, the next the sergeant-major was by his side.

'What the hell's going on in there?' Dai Williams asked. 'You're in and out like a bloody jack-in-a-box.'

'The shits, sir,' Jim said, 'we've all got the shits something awful. I think you'd better go and talk to them. I'll stay out here. If I can.'

'What do you mean, if you can? If necessary, you'll shit your pants, and that's an order . . .' The sergeant-major crawled through the bushes. Frank who'd been behind the hut followed him inside.

'You've all got it . . .?' No need to ask; they were doubled in agony clutching their guts.

'Thank your lucky stars you were first on guard,' Freddie said, 'otherwise you'd have eaten some of that M&V with the rest of us.' The sergeant-major smelled what was left of the stew in the mess-tin, which, thoughtfully, they'd saved for him. It stank rancid. 'Bloody fools to eat that lot in the first place,' he said, but he knew it wasn't their fault.

What they needed was a bottle of good, old-fashioned jollop. Something to concrete 'em up inside. Unless what they'd got was actual salmonella. They could die from that, very quickly.

'Right lads, I'll be back as quick as I can. Stuff your handkerchiefs into your mouths so you won't groan out loud.'

'We'd do better with corks up our arses.'

He went rapidly out of the back of the hut. No time to waste. Along the back of the shrubberies to the clipped cut in the fence. Opened it carefully, ducked out. Nobody watching. The plan was bad; they ought to have set up a channel of communication between the captain and himself; it was bad practice to keep out of touch this way. Dammit, anything could happen. But who could have predicted food poisoning?

Down the side of the Parc, watching. Curfew was on. If anyone saw him they'd pick him up immediately. He cut across the avenue, in among the houses. He remembered seeing a pharmacy in one of the roads in which they'd planted the mines. Hug the sides of the buildings. Move slowly, but as quick as possible. He ducked into doorways a couple of times when mobile patrols came past on motor-cycle combinations. Round a corner, into the street. There it was. Shuttered, locked-up of course. In a four-storey build-ing, an alleyway alongside it. The alleyway was blocked by a wooden door. Too public here to mess about. He could be caught easily if a patrol came along. He walked along the street counting his steps to the end of the block of buildings which contained the pharmacy and went round to the back of the buildings. A long, narrow alleyway. Oh Christ, no possibility of concealment; once committed to that alley-way, he had a hundred yards to go, and anyone checking along it would be bound to see him. He walked forward. It'd been eighty paces from the pharmacy; he traced eighty back, every pace a nerve-tingling fear of a machine-gun death coming out of the dark at him. This must be about right. Wooden fence six feet high on each side. He looked over, to the left. Ten yards farther, then quick, over the fence. This is what you've trained for, fast, silent movement in the dark. Boxes stacked up in the back-yard, cardboard and wood. They'd be using them again, salvaging every-thing. Small yard, about twenty feet by thirty across. Back door, shuttered. No doubt a bolt, locks; forget it. Back win-dow down to the ground. Shuttered again, regular fortress. Forget that too. Bog window. That's more like it. Metal window with crinkly glass in it. Window's rusted. Open an eighth of an inch one side. Tips of his fingers. No use. Knife. Slide it along first to clear the paintwork, if there's any left; takes time but it's worth it. Two hinges thick with paint and what feels like old putty. Chisel it away. Knife blade under the window and lever, praying to the God of Wales, the special God that makes people leave lavatory windows slightly ajar and forget to lock them. The window creaked open a quarter of an inch. Wait and listen. Listen and wait. Silence. Who'd think that he, Dai Williams, that pillar of rectitude, would be burgling a shop? Fingers under the lip of the window and pull. Bugger the noise if you make it quick and don't follow up with other noises. Quick pull, window's open. It screeched like hell. Stand absolutely still. No sound. Hands inside the window frame. Good, there's a lip. Hold the lip and pull upwards, arms through the window, twist your body, tight fit but you'll make it easy, don't fall over or you'll finish up with your head down the lavatory pan. Psychosomatic, but the thought of the lavatory, the memory of the lads all hunched up, gave him a pain in the gut. He found the bracket of the cistern, tested it, then used it to draw himself through the window and into the lavatory. If the door's locked . . . ? But it wasn't. And it wasn't a lavatory pan, either, just a hole in the floor. He went through the back of the pharmacy. No doors locked. Into the shop itself, the universal odour of pharmacies everywhere. But where's the anti-shit? Millions of bottles, millions of cupboards, or so it seemed. He was carrying a flat torch, switched it on cautiously. The big, bubble eye was taped, so that only a crossed beam shone out. He directed it on the floor, walked over to the windows. The shutters outside seemed light proof, but you can never tell. Bottles everywhere, tubes of ointment everywhere.

Finally he found something that looked suitable. Against nausea, vomiting, and the evils of the stomach. A liquid in a brown bottle. He opened it and sniffed. That was it, a French version of jollop. It was milky, but the liquid was brown. Smelled of chlorodyne. That's it, chalk and chlorodyne, kaolin and opium. Liquid concrete. Blocked you up while the chlorodyne soothed the pain in the stomach linings. He took five bottles.

Distributed them about his pockets. Was going out through the back of the shop when the lights came on. Quick look about. No one. No one standing there with a pistol looking at him, saying put your hands up. Quick. Duck through to the back. He was already in the lavatory when he heard the slippers slapping on the staircase from the flat above, heard a quivering voice saying. *'Qui est là?'*

He didn't answer. Out through the window in one long heave that dropped him to the ground outside, silent as a big cat. He rolled over and up, streaked out to the fence, up and over backwards, just in case someone's waiting the other side. No one. Risk it, run along the alleyway. End. Turn right. Into the street of the pharmacy. Walk slowly, hugging the walls. This is the dangerous bit. What if the shop-owner used the telephone before he got brave and switched on the shop light from the head of the stairs, afraid to descend into the black?

No evidence of any disturbance behind the shutters, though he could see now they weren't light proof. Two thin pencil beams probed across the pavement. Hit the far wall, picked it out with light. The sergeant-major flattened himself against the buildings, trapped. He'd have to go through those light rays. Into a doorway and think. No use crouching. Then he heard the phut-phut of an engine. In trouble. Back, back against the door.

A motor-cycle combination comes round the corner, its engine spluttering. Damn. It stops short of the pencil rays. Dies. The driver kicks it. It won't start. His passenger gets out to stretch his legs, looking at the bike, muttering. The driver gets off, checks the plug cap is firmly fixed. Scratches the back of his neck, looks at the engine as if it is the first he's ever seen. The passenger crouches beside him, pointing. The driver shakes his head.

The sergeant-major makes up his mind, comes out of the doorway, turns left, walks along the edge of the pavement, against the buildings, on the balls of his feet. Knife in his right hand, the other held out slightly to the front and at the side for balance, to provide impulsion if he needs to move fast. Glides along, not breaking the motion into separate steps. And prays for silence. Feet down heel and toe, the quiet way. Both men tinkering but, most importantly, *looking* at the defunct engine. Fear sharpens the senses. The sergeant-major can smell the burned oil stink of the engine. Ray of light across the street.

Peripheral vision's a curious thing, some people have it, some don't. If either one of the Germans has it, he'll spot the sergeant-major the second that light hits him. The passenger has his Schmeisser in his hand. Try to get past and take a chance? If you know you're going to do a thing your mind prepared everything. So, change the plan. Don't tell yourself you're going to try to get past them. You're going to take them. That way, you'll go for them hard and fast, with a better hope of success than if you try to slide past and have to change the plan at the last second because that Schmeisser's spitting at you. Tense, prepared, ready, *go*. Straight through the light beam in one continuous motion and across the road. Right to change plan. One of them has good side vision. The passenger flicks his head and his Schmeisser follows the motion. Go. Forward and low, blood pumping, legs working. Forget small noise caution, right hand back, no, quick flip to change the knife right to left and arm drawn back to body level and one movement forward as the knife goes under the German's elbow, past his hand fumbling for the safety catch of the Schmeisser which he never gets off since the sudden, shocking pain of that knife going in blanches his cheeks which start to sag, and the sergeant-major's right hand already curving in a vicious arc towards the neck of the driver crouched over the machine and the driver sensing but not hearing, feeling but not knowing, jerks up his head and his steel helmet covers the nape of his neck and the side of the sergeant's hand, the hardened sharpened side clunks against the curve of the back of the steel helmet and the sergeant-major feels as if he'd dashed his hand into concrete. The driver's face smashes forward against the flanged side of the engine, the overheated metal, and he slumps and his face drags against the starter pedal which lifts his upper lip in a grimace before it releases him to fall flat on the ground, his face a mess of blood and oil and grease.

By that time, the sergeant-major, nursing his right hand, has turned the corner out of the street.

CHAPTER TEN

I was looking out of the window again. At last, Heidi had gone to sleep. Soon it would be dawn, and then the busy day, the end of the long fuse that would explode into life at seven o'clock that evening, when the *'Stimme aus Berlin'* was reincarnated. Dai and the lads would already be in the Parc. I trusted Dai completely to have done his job. The fuses would already be laid to blow all approaches to the Parc at seven o'clock that evening. Henk would be working quietly in the telephone exchange, ready to create his own kind of chaos. He'd been incredulous when our courier, now hiding in St Avold with the radio, had given him the details of our scheme. The brigadier was a damned efficient, painstaking planner. He'd got together the best men from three London telephone exchanges to work that one out, and it was so simple. Henk would have no problems; apparently he was good at his job.

Heidi stirred, murmured softly, and I walked quietly across to the side of the bed, pulled the sheet and the blanket up round her shoulders. She needed sleep; she'd told me a night without sleep always revealed itself in her voice, and in dark rings under her eyes. There'd be dark rings tomorrow. No, today.

Of course, I never could have killed her. The brigadier must have seen that. But he'd hope I'd be able to frighten her with what I believed to be a genuine threat. Killing a woman in the abstract sounds no harder than killing a man, once you've trained yourself to accept that either one of them is a hunk of meat standing in your way. But now that I had met her, now that I had seen her, and spoken with her, and knew she had a private existence outside the demands of war, I could not kill her.

I told myself I didn't need to; if she impeded us we could do without her. We could knock her out, tie her up, make other plans for the broadcast. There might even be recordings of the programme, in which case we could lift her opening anouncement and use that to start the broadcast. If necesssary we could pre-record Hinton's voice, though I'd taken the brigadier's point of view that it was better if Hinton broadcast 'live', if the listeners could have a sense of Hinton being actually there in the studio while he was speaking. Its impact would be diminished unless the broadcast was totally credible, unless the listener could be convinced Hinton had risked his life to get to the studio to make it.

CHAPTER ELEVEN

John was on guard. The jollop had worked, at least temporarily. After the sergeant-major had gone he'd swigged another quarter of the bottle. Ugh, chalk and chlorodyne. But it worked.

He was squatting beneath an evergreen, his knees bent, his gun in his hand. From there he could see the guard-house on the gate. Nothing else moved in the Parc, except morning mist that rolled over the grass. Funny, the way he'd taken to the life. Once upon a time he'd have been dead scared without buildings all about him. What was it the quack had called it, agoraphobia? It had nearly done for him in those early days, out on the moors, with not a building in sight. Him, who'd spent all his life in small rooms, in narrow streets. Damn it, he'd even felt sick in Hyde Park, looking after a couple of girls who took 'em in the bushes. As for going into the bushes himself – nah, you'd never get him doing that. Give him a hot, smoky room, smell of booze, human beings, fags, sweat, a band playing in the corner or a piano, and some bird to chat up. That was his paradise. Johnnie the Pimp, but was he happy. 'Want a bird? I'll get you one. What colour hair? Want a box o' fags, off a lorry? Cost you ten quid. Bottle of whisky at five o'clock in the morning? Sure. But it'll cost you.' And then the Army, and the great outdoors. Remember the first time on leave. Down in Whitechapel. 'Look at the man, you'd take him for a soldier.' But there was respect, wasn't there? People buying him drinks, not so's he'd get 'em a bird, but out of respect. And the lads. Talked to him for a change, instead of telling him to poof off. Nobody likes a pimp, somehow. Well, they didn't think that way any more. Last time he'd been home, with his beret on, and his jumper's wings, he'd had 'em falling down in front of him, saying, 'take me now, you gorgeous hunk of man'. And, of course, he was a hunk o' man, wasn't he? He'd put on two stones, all on his chest and his biceps. Now he had muscles. Dammit, his cock had even grown bigger, or was that an illusion? He laughed to himself. Don't say the Army had given him muscles there, as well.

Activity in the guard house. All four of 'em, looking down the road, opening the bloody gates. What's coming in? Nobody comes in here during the night. Waste of time keeping the guard out of their wankers.

Jesus bloody Christ! The bloody Army's arrived! The whole, bloody, German Army.

CHAPTER TWELVE

I went into the kitchen and made David Hinton a cup of tea, put it on a saucer, even changed the saucer and wiped the bottom of the cup when I spilled a drop. I skimmed off the inevitable powder-specks that always made the pre-fabricated brew look fly-specked and unwholesome. Then I shook his shoulder gently.

He was instantly awake. 'Ah, tea. Thanks awfully.' He took it in his hands and drank it in one fast gulp. He put the cup back on the saucer, and I returned to the kitchen. When I came back he'd gone into the bathroom and had shut the door behind him.

When he came out again he'd washed and must have

wetted his hair before he brushed it back. 'Thanks for the tea,' he said.

'That's all right, David,' I said.

'You called me David,' he said, 'and that's the first time. Any particular reason why?'

I shook my head. He glanced into the bedroom where Heidi lay asleep. 'Get any sleep yourself, Captain?' I felt it was the first time he'd called me Captain voluntarily without denigrating the rank. I shook my head again. 'Sleep doesn't bother me too much when I'm on a job.'

'I envy you that,' he said. 'I suppose I've been spoiled, but I do seem to need to nod off occasionally.' His speech was affected, but for the first time I realized that each of us speaks the language of his environment, and he was no more to blame for the way he spoke than John was for the way he swore all the time. It'd been a long night, and I'd been thinking a lot about David Hinton.

Something Heidi had said set me off. Hinton was just obeying his individual conscience when he broadcast for the Germans. He believed in what he was doing. Of course, I could think he was wrong, but it was his privilege to think he was right. Could I be absolutely certain that there was no grain of truth in what he'd said in his *Stimme aus Berlin* broadcasts, that chaps like me were being used as cannon fodder to perpetuate a class power structure in which we had no rights, no privileges? They were paying lip service to democracy, of course, with the coalition government, but could I truly believe that either side of that uneasy liason consisted of men who had ultimate, long-term good in view?

'I've been a bit shirty with you, David, from time to time, and I'd like to apologize.'

'Just getting everything square, eh, before we go over the top?'

'Not exactly. Getting it out of my system.'

He was thoughtful for a moment. 'You don't like this job, do you?' he asked. 'Nothing to do with me, or your feelings about me. To do with the job itself?'

'I don't like any job, the success of which could depend

on our ability to murder a woman. A sentry, yes; a hundred soldiers, yes. But not a woman.'

'I know it's a bit of a cliché, but she's a soldier, too. Comforts for the troops and all that.'

'I can't see it in that light. To me she's a woman.'

'And you don't believe in loving 'em and leaving 'em?'

'Do you? Is that your personal philosophy . . .?'

He laughed, but for once I took no offence from it. 'God, no,' he said. 'I don't have a philosophy about women. The progress of civilization has been perverted from time to time by a woman seizing the reins – Cleopatra, Catherine the Great, Elizabeth – the one thing they had in common was a fervent nationalism. The root of our evil is not women but nationalism – arbitrary divisions of the world into little parcels of land, each to be defended to the death. What people can't see is that no country has a prerogative for right. And that's the nearest thing to a philosophy I'll admit to at this time of the morning. Now, Captain, why don't you get some sleep? I'll stand guard.'

Now I felt I could trust him.

For the first time I felt he'd do the job for which I'd brought him, and do it well. I'd lost my hatred for him, washed away during the long night, waiting for the dawn.

'I think I will have a couple of hours,' I said.

He stripped the blanket from the bed, shook it, folded it neatly for me, and laid it on the horse-hair sofa.

I could hear an engine in the street. It had a familiar sound. I held up my hand to silence him, went towards the window. Before I got there, two brief horn blasts. Pause. Two more brief horn blasts.

'François,' I said. 'Can you cope?'

He nodded.

'Let her sleep,' I said, as I went out of the door, fast. Down the stairs, silently as possible. No one was there. No one at the door. Turn left, walk down the street to the corner. The lorry was parked just round the corner, the men in a bar. '*Un verre de blanc, s'il vous plaît.*' François, and Czeslaw. Took my glass, stood there drinking from it.

'*Allons-y,*' François called, '*on est pressé, allons-y . . .*'

The men put down their glasses and swept out of the bar, me in the centre. Up onto the back of the lorry. Grasp a spade, stand there while the lorry moved off. François standing beside me.

'Trouble?' I asked.

'The worst.'

'Where?'

'You'd better come and look.'

The lorry drove along the avenues. Not much traffic about. We passed the scenes of two of last night's 'explosions'. I flinched as the lorry drove over the manhole I knew had been spiked. Damn it, I'd studied photographs François had supplied and knew the street backwards. At the far end of the street we turned left into another. That one was also mined. The large building behind me, with *MEUBLES* carved in stone over the doorway. It was coming down this evening I hoped, in a neat one-act demolition. At seven o'clock.

At the end of the street, the avenue that ran along the side of the Parc. No way into that avenue this evening, with all its approaches mined. An infantry detachment had already started to erect dark green bell tents across the lawn of the Parc des Ouvriers. I counted fifteen lorries, each capable of carrying thirty men. Four hundred and fifty soldiers. Infantry. An ambulance, no, two ambulances. A Field Headquarters Section. Field kitchens with smoke already beginning to rise out of the funnels. The one thing we hadn't planned for. An Army unit, camping out in the Parc. The lorry didn't stop but coasted slowly parallel with the wire.

'Where are my men?' I asked François.

'In the Parc. In the hut, I imagine.'

'How long has this lot been here?'

'An hour.'

'Who are they, where are they from?'

'I don't know. We can find out from Henk. They're bound to put in a telephone centre ...'

'If they plan to stay. Perhaps they're only here until ten past seven.'

'Impossible. Who could know?'

'You know. Your lot knows.'

'Your man in St Avold; he knows. Avalon, he knew.'

'Will you vouch for your men?'

'Absolutely. With my life. Every one of them. Will you vouch for yours?'

Would I? One of them was a murderer. One of them was Hinton. Would I vouch for Hinton? Would I vouch for a murderer? 'Yes, I'll vouch for them,' I said.

'Then it has to be a coincidence. Not a plan. So, what do we do? We can't land a plane while they are there, can we? So we can't get you out.'

'That's not too important. We can always walk home if we have to. But we can't risk going into that station. Hinton has to make his broadcast and it has to be completed and uninterrupted for maximum effect. If any German can get to the studio while Hinton is broadcasting, and can shoot him on the air, or stop the broadcast, it will merely reinforce the invincibility of the Glorious Reich. In a highly dramatic way that'll appeal to every person listening. With all those soldiers, some of them are bound to hear the broadcast, and if they do, they can get to the studio in minutes. Look at that little lot, it's not a fishing rod.'

It was a high-frequency aerial fixed to the top of a truck. Through that radio link, the Gestapo could get at them within seconds, undoing all the confusion Henk would have created with his telephones.

'Where is your transmitter?' I asked François.

'We don't like to tell that information to anyone. I'm the only one, apart from the operator, who knows, now that Avalon is dead. Anyway, what do you want to transmit? If they come and bomb the Parc, to get the soldiers out, you'll never land a plane there. And you certainly won't move the soldiers.'

'Take me to the transmitter.'

He hesitated: that transmitter was the heart of the Maquis for the region. If that were given away, no more calls to England; no more supplies, rifles, pistols, ammunition, fuses, detonators, extra food, maps, clothing, all the things we regularly supplied. 'I need that transmitter,' I said, 'I *need* it.'

Something in my voice must have convinced him. He bent over the side of the lorry, said something to the man in the cab. The lorry turned into a side street, reversed out, blocking the path of a German soldier in a side-car combination. The soldier cursed. The men on the back shouted at him, '*Ministère des Travaux Publiques.* There's an unexploded bomb ahead . . .' It was one of their more effective jokes. The combination turned rapidly round, went racing back up the street. The lorry went along past about fifty houses, then stopped. François beckoned for me to jump over the side, then he followed me. He said something to the driver, and the lorry drove off.

'It's here,' François said, 'in this building. We keep it here because it's so near to the Radio Strasbourg transmitter. Too near for the direction finders to locate it . . .'

We climbed into the building. A block of apartments, similar in style to Heidi's, though less clean, lower class. The narrow staircase smelled of cabbage and urine. We went to the top of the house, knocked on a door. It sounded like a normal knock. After a minute or so we heard shuffling behind the door. '*Wer da?*' a voice asked, the voice of an old man.

'François.'

The door was old and appeared to be cracked, but I could see the Judas eye, built neatly into the crack, through which the old man inside would be scanning the hall.

I stood away from François, my hands in full view and empty. The door opened. An old man stood there.

François introduced me. 'This is my uncle,' he told me, 'and this is a comrade.'

The radio was in the roof. With Heloise. My heart sank when I saw her. About my age and pretty. I needed a technician.

François must have seen something of the disappointment on my face when he introduced us. He laughed. 'Don't worry,' he said, 'Heloise knows all there is to know about radios. Believe me. She was building them – how do you call it, with the cat's whiskers when other girls were playing with dolls.' I groaned when I saw the radio. It looked as if it still used cat's whiskers. It was certainly like no radio I'd ever seen before. And what we had to do was highly technical.

'Can you fit a direction-finding aerial to that machine?'

'I have one already.' Surprise number one.

'If you were looking for a low-power transmitter, and I couldn't give you its wavelength, or its signal, only its exact location, could you find it?'

'You mean, the one in the Parc des Ouvriers?' she said, smiling. Surprise number two. 'I've had them since they went on the air about fifty minutes ago. They're using radio telephone.'

'So, they're purely local. Where are they broadcasting to?'

'A two-way link with Brigade. Almost due North. From the signal strength I'd estimate Brigade to be at Haguenau.'

'No communication with the Headquarters of the Gestapo, here in Strasbourg?'

She shook her head. 'They wouldn't have,' she said. 'The Gestapo is very particular who it nets with. They want to keep their frequencies clear. Assuming the Gestapo wanted to communicate with the Parc the normal route would be local Gestapo to Brigade Gestapo – Brigade Gestapo to Brigade – Brigade to the Parc.'

'Seems a long way round . . .'

'You know the Teutonic mind.'

'Why is the Parc using voices, not morse keys? That must cut the range.'

'Often happens with a newly set up station. Set up on voice, switch to morse when the important message starts. I haven't been monitoring them all the time, but they were passing routine "setting-up" messages when I did listen.'

'Any idea of the reason for being here?'

'Nothing is being said about that.'

'Can you switch 'em on for me?' She went to the corner of the room, switched on the radio. I waited for it to warm up, impatient. After two minutes or so I could hear the hum of the amplifier. It was surprisingly quiet. She saw my expression. 'I'm going to make a living with that after the war,' she said. 'I can cut down signal to noise ratio. My own circuit, and very easy to mass produce. I shall sell it to somebody like Philips of Eindhoven, or His Master's Voice . . .' We waited. Suddenly the set started to hum. 'Carrier wave,' she said. She pressed a couple of switches, the set made a shrieking noise, and she tuned it slowly by turning a dial so that the high-pitched whistle became a soft-burbling sound then disappeared altogether. 'Beat frequency oscillator?' I asked. Just to air what little knowledge I had. 'Yes,' she said, 'the operator in the Parc isn't too experienced. He always presses his switch before he starts to sort out what he's going to say.' A voice came on the loudspeaker. The message was routine. Call sign, identification sign. Message specifying kitchen stores to be delivered the following day at 12.00 hours.

The distant station, of which this was a satellite, was sending by morse key. Very professional, but obviously held back in speed to give this operator a chance. 'How long do you think they'll need to pack up that camp and go?' I asked François.

'Pack it up completely?'

'Completely. Starting from scratch.'

He thought. Out loud. 'Fifteen trucks of men, that's approximately four hundred and fifty men, that's roughly sixty bell tents. Field kitchen, headquarters, signals section. Clean up. I'd allow them at least two hours to get out of here.'

'And then to get out of Strasbourg?'

'Convoy, thirty troop trucks plus the rest. You'd need to give them at least forty-five minutes from the first vehicle leaving the Parc to the last vehicle crossing the river bridge. At least forty-five minutes.'

I wrote a message on a pad. Very carefully. 'Think you can send that,' I said to Heloise, 'with your output gain turned down to give you a limited reach, say five miles?'

She read the message, and her face lit up.

'Yes, I think I can . . .'

'Don't think, know. Do you *know* you can? Morse, of course.'

'I can even imitate the way he uses the key,' she said.

'Good. Send that message for me. At exactly 15.45 hours. *Wilco?*'

'*Wilco*, Roger, whichever way you want it,' she said. She handed me a small satchel. 'Take this with you,' she said. 'A little something else I've invented, and am saving until after the war.'

'What is it?'

'A portable radio. It works off the lorry battery,' she said. 'François will show you how. You'll be able to listen in to my broadcast. At 15.45 hours.'

CHAPTER THIRTEEN

Heidi traced the outline of David Hinton's nose with her finger, and her hand continued down his face onto his chest. Playfully she tugged at one of the hairs on his chest. His eyes opened.

'Your Captain,' she said, 'has a conscience.'

'He's not MY captain,' he said, 'I take no responsibility for him.'

'If he comes back unexpectedly . . . ?'

'I've jammed the door.'

'You think of everything.'

'And you'd better think of everything if we're going to carry this thing through.'

'How do I know you won't change your mind . . . ?'

'You don't know, do you?'

'How do I know you won't double-cross me . . . ?'

'You can't know, can you? But ask yourself this one question. Why would I take you into my confidence if I didn't need you?'

'Good question. I don't have an answer.'

She rolled over until she was half on top of him, their

naked bodies locked closely together. 'I shan't be able to see you afterwards,' she said, 'you realize that?'

'Yes, you will. I won't always be in Berlin. Anyway, you'll have your Luftwaffe pilot . . .'

'You heard that? You weren't asleep.'

'Not for one second . . .'

'Peeping Tom.'

'Peeping Jill – what about when he was baring his heart to me, when he'd given me that cup of tea?'

'I almost died, holding my laugh in . . .'

'I can imagine. Look, while you're on top, why not do to me, eh? Change of place, change of pace, and all that.'

'One thing he was right about,' she said, her eyes glittering with the pleasure of anticipation, 'you *use* women.'

'How can you say that?' he said. 'You're the one who's using me, right now. And if you stop, I shall *certainly* kill you.'

CHAPTER FOURTEEN

Heidi's street was deserted. The car outside the front of her apartment block stood out like a sore thumb. I walked slowly along the street from the corner where François had dropped me, too far away to see if the car was occupied. Look up at the windows. Nothing shows. Never does, does it? Glass reflects the light, and the reflection can hide an army of eyes. If it's a trap . . . Would they leave the car parked outside? Who can tell? A Luftwaffe pilot, come home early? The man who was protecting Heidi, whoever he may be?

I forced myself to walk on, close to the building, keeping a natural pace. But ready to drop to the ground should a Spandau chatter at me. Forward. Natural. Neither too slow nor too fast. Body tingling, already anticipating the thud of bullets. It's the impact that hurts, like banging your knee on

a sharp corner. Hands in my pocket holding the Colt automatic. Useless at that range. Close up it's a stopper, but the
range is too long. Drawing closer. Can see inside the car.
No one visible. Doesn't mean no one is in there. I'd squat in
the well by the back seat, with my Schmeisser resting between the two front seats. If it were me . . . Twenty-five
yards to go. Committed now. No sense in dropping to the
ground. This is a job for a grenade. But I haven't got a
grenade. Car has a bump on the front wing. Rusted metal
shows through the paint. No sign of anyone inside. Doorways and windows of the buildings. Street fighting's a pants-
filling business if you're the one in the street. Fifteen yards
away. Commitment total. Too late even for 'Our Father . . .'
The car is a shooting-brake-type Mercedes; a high radiator
at the end of a long bonnet. A haughty car. Low down on
its back springs. Age, or the weight of three of four hefty SS
men? Nearer. The clank of my feet on the pavement. Rubbish, you're imagining. Without Innsbrucker soles my boots
are silent as carpet slippers. Something in the back of the
car, covered with a black cloth. Something bulky. I bring the
gun out of my pocket in the palm of my hand, pull back the
slide to cock it, hold my other hand over my gun to mask it.
One up the spout, safety catch off. No, Colts don't work
like that. One waiting to go up the spout and be fired. Here's
the car. Level with it. Go down the street, or into Heidi's
building? How to decide? They could be hiding in the back
of the shooting-brake. If I go down the street I get it in the
back. I turn into the building, run up the stairs.

The door to Heidi's apartment was open. A piece of string
had been looped round the knob on both sides, preventing
the door from catching. I could hear voices inside. Hinton's
voice, quite clear, talking easy. No sign of tension. Using his
normal voice, so that was okay. If he was in trouble, he'd
switch to another German accent.

They were sitting round the table. Three of them. Hinton,
Heidi, and a small man. Hinton rose quickly to his feet. 'Ah
Franz,' he said, 'I'm glad you got back so quickly. Now
you can see something interesting. But first, may I present
Herr Stocheln, from the broadcasting station.'

'*MONSIEUR Stocheln, s'il vous plaît,*' Stocheln said, simpering.

He extended his hand and I took it. I dared not shake it in case it slipped through my fingers. It was cold and wet, like a cod's back. Stocheln was a simperer, the worst kind. '*Enchanté,*' he said when I let his hand drop. 'He is my cousin,' Hinton said by way of explanation. 'We both came to see our cousin Heidi, before we go to Frankfurt tomorrow.'

'Both on leave at the same time? How fortunate. But now, alas, I hope you will forgive me if I continue the recording. I am only supposed to work until twelve o'clock, and then I must get started on my voyage.'

'Going far, Monsieur Stocheln?' I asked casually.

'To Colmar.' Voyage, indeed. Colmar is only sixty kilometres from Strasbourg.

'Was that your car I saw outside?'

'No, it is a recording car of the broadcasting station. Today I drive to Colmar; tomorrow I make recordings in a camp. I mustn't tell you which camp,' he simpered, 'that's a military secret. But I am to record soldiers' voices for our evening programme, *Wass Sie Wollen.*'

'A request programme . . .?'

'Yes; pick a piece of music and we play it for you.'

'What an unusual idea, don't you think, Franz?' Hinton said. 'And Herr, I'm sorry, *Monsieur* Stocheln, doesn't have the time to return to the studio before he departs for Colmar.'

Message received and understood. No danger here. Stocheln isn't going back to the studio, won't mention having seen us here. Okay, but the bastard can use the telephone, can't he?

'Perhaps Monsieur Stocheln could give our friend a lift? You know, the one who's going to Sélestat. It's on the way to Colmar. . .' So we'd get one of François's men to go with him, to make certain he didn't use the telephone.

Now Heidi got the message. She walked to the window and I followed her. 'Let's get one thing straight,' she whispered so that Stocheln couldn't hear. 'I wouldn't like anything to happen to Stocheln. I'd need your promise.' I nodded. Stocheln didn't interest me except as a possible source of danger.

'He and our friend will get on well together. I promise you.'

No violence, but no telephone calls.

Stocheln had come to record Heidi's introduction to the programme they were doing next week. I watched him use the recording machine set up in the kitchen. Very simple. Nothing to it. Shut the kitchen door, switch on, wait for it all to warm up, put a blank on the machine, a disc with an acetate surface. Lower the head onto the acetate, and its needle cuts a groove. A small suction head drew the thin cutting of swarf away from the cutting head, and left a clean acetate disc. As soon as the groove had started to cut properly, he tapped on the door. Heidi heard him, waited five seconds, and then began to speak. We could hear her voice through a speaker attached to the recording machine.

When she'd finished speaking, she waited a few seconds. Stocheln worked a handle that spiralled the cut groove to the centre of the acetate disc, and then he lifted the cutting needle. Bob's your uncle. One gramophone record. One switch intrigued me. 'What's that?' I asked him.

He loved explaining things. 'That's the prefade switch,' he said. 'Three positions. If you put it up, we are listening to the actual microphone. If you put it down we are listening to the actual groove of the record being played, *after* it had been cut.'

'You said, three positions?'

'Ah yes, we don't use the third one at the moment. But if we were broadcasting live from this place, using it as a studio, we could either be listening to the voice on the microphone, or to a gramophone that was being played, or to what was actually going out on the air.'

'And they might not be the same?'

'Of course not. Miss Lotl could have prerecorded part of her programme. I'd have it in here on the disc. She could be in the studio, rehearsing her next "live" broadcast. On pre-fade, I'd be listening to the output, which would be from the gramophone record, not live from the studio.'

We made a phone call and Czeslaw was the man François sent. Complete with a small suitcase he looked the perfect weekender. 'Your papers are in order, I suppose?' Stocheln said, the professional worrier.

I wasn't surprised to find the papers included a permit to travel to Sélestat that day, by road or rail. Stocheln left the recordings with Heidi, fussing even when she promised to deliver them safely when she went for her broadcast. As soon as they had left the apartment she turned to me. 'That man won't hurt Stocheln, will he? I have your word for that.'

'You have my word. He'll only stop Stocheln if he tries to use the telephone. He must surely have recognized David Hinton as the *"Stimme aus Berlin"*. Presumably a recording engineer develops a good memory for voices.'

'Yes, he recognized me as soon as I spoke. I told him I was incognito. That I'd been in hospital suffering from shell-shock, and didn't want word to get around. I told him that, for a time, I'd been in the mental ward . . .'

'Was that wise? He strikes me as a man who loves to gossip. Especially about a thing like that.'

'Let him gossip. To Czeslaw. Look, when he came to the door I had no alternative but to let him in. He recognized my voice immediately, and my face soon after, from the publicity pictures.'

'You knew he was coming . . .?' I said to Heidi.

'I'd forgotten.'

'How many others have you conveniently "forgotten"? How many other people are going to turn up here today?'

She shook her head. 'I didn't want him here any more than you did. It's bad enough risking my own life, without involving other innocent people. I wanted to get him out of your way, as quickly as possible. For his own sake.'

Something was wrong. A bond had been formed between her and Hinton. I could sense he was on her side, not mine. She seemed somehow defiant, with a new inner strength.

'You should have been here to cope,' Hinton said. 'What kept you?'

'It was a beautiful morning. I thought I'd take a stroll...'

And that was all the answer he was going to get out of me. I have a nose for situations; this one had gone wrong. Okay, they were two skilled broadcasters, and that gave them a common interest, a bond I couldn't share. They were social equals and I was outside that zone of privilege. But, probably most importantly, they were two subordinates, and I was the man in charge, and they banded together against authority. So I decided to exercise that authority, to take out an insurance.

In a rack above the recording machine in the kitchen was a packet of new acetate blanks. I opened it and slipped one on the machine, which I switched on to allow it to warm up again. 'Right, David, sit at the table with the microphone in the normal position, and say something. Go on talking until I tell you to stop.'

He sat down, adjusted the microphone, a true professional, then started to speak. I lowered the cutting head onto the acetate the way I had seen Stocheln do it, picked up the start of the swarf with the camel hair brush the way he had, and fed it into the suction. Then I took the playback head and placed it on the acetate disc in the groove the recording had cut. When I joggled the prefade switch I could hear what Hinton was saying, and what had been recorded a second or two before. The recording was perfectly clear. I lifted the playing head and the cutting head and examined the acetate disc. It seemed perfectly all right, even when compared with the test cut Stocheln had made earlier that day.

I had the brigadier's script. 'Now we'll record that,' I said. He looked at me, looked at her. 'We'll record it, and I'll carry the record with me, so that if at the last moment, you happen to slip and sprain your larynx, I've still got your immortal words. For posterity and the Glory of the Third Reich.' He looked at the script.

'I cannot record it, just like that,' he said, 'I need time to work on it first.'

'So far as I'm concerned, the brigadier has already done all the work that's necessary on that text. I want it recorded without a single word being changed. And that, not that you care over much, is an order, Private Hinton.' I took the Colt .45 out of my pocket, cocked it by pulling back the slide.

'You wouldn't dare shoot in here,' Heidi said.

I flipped the knife from my sleeve, held it by the handle, and flipped it. It stuck in the side of Hinton's chair, a half an inch from his arm. I walked across and plucked the knife out of the chair.

'I wouldn't need to shoot,' I said.

Give Hinton credit. He never flinched. I was a bully, and showing off, but he wouldn't flinch. Not so Heidi. She put her fist to her mouth when she saw how close the knife had gone, how deeply it had stuck into the chair. She knew I could pin Hinton or her to the back of the chairs in which they were sitting, faster than they could move. They say that, with a good throw, the knife leaves your hand at sixty miles an hour.

'Right, Private Hinton, we'll start the recording as soon as you're ready. And you Fräulein Lotl, can be an appreciative audience of one. In the kitchen. Move.'

She did. No looking back either in place or time. No looking back at Hinton sitting in the chair, no looking back to the bright-eyed girl who, a few short hours ago, had said, 'I want you to make love to me.' I hadn't fallen for that one. Perhaps Hinton had, after I'd left. Perhaps that was the bond they held between them. I followed her into the kitchen, confident Hinton would do nothing to provoke me and endanger her. I could hear him mumbling the words of the script. The brigadier had given me a copy. I opened it and placed it in a clip above the recording machine.

'Sit down in that corner,' I said to Heidi, 'and put your hands on your lap where I can see them. She sat on the floor, pulling her robe modestly round her legs stretched out in front of her. She folded her hands on her lap. I put the gun in my pocket, the knife back up my sleeve. 'Right, keep quiet, Hinton,' I shouted.

'Damn it, I need more time,' he said.

I knew that was a load of balls; the brigadier told me he'd made Hinton memorize the script in case the paper should get lost, or he had to do the broadcast in the dark. 'I'm going to shut this door. Start when I bang on it.

I shut the door, started the cutting head on a new blank, banged on the door, and his voice started, firm and confident. No doubt about it, he was a natural broadcaster. It was a good script the brigadier had supplied. It identified David Hinton as the *'Stimme aus Berlin'*, the man who'd been deceived by the events in Germany prior to the war, who'd returned to England and seen for himself how the free world lived. Then it went on to give details of atrocities committed against the Jews and the Poles. It named individual officers, gave exact locations of camps. It was a damning indictment of the Nazi war machine, skilfully compiled from Intelligence sources. It told the German people in clear, unmistakable, easily-provable statements that, if the present war machine continued, there would be no future on earth for any member of the German nation. The recording took four acetate discs altogether. By the time I was on the last one, Heidi was standing beside me, showing me how to cut off the microphone at the end of a sentence neatly. How to stop Hinton, start him again at the beginning of the next sentence so that the discs could be played successively, with no pause apparent on the air. Frankly, I could never have told that the speech was recorded. Hinton did it so easily, so naturally, pausing when he appeared to be searching for a word, speaking the names and locations as though reading them from a dossier. He even rustled his script in the right places, to suggest he was holding a signed and sealed attestation of the accuracy of his remarks.

During the recording, Heidi didn't seem interested in the content of what he said, only the professional technique. When it was ended she rushed into the sitting-room. 'That was marvellous,' she said, as if he'd just performed Hamlet.

'Was it all right?' Hinton asked me, his professional pleasure and need for reassurance overcoming his hatred of me.

'Just what the doctor ordered . . .'

'You mean the brigadier . . .'

I wrapped the discs in bags, then placed them inside the case I'd been carrying. They were a tight fit, but at least they wouldn't be damaged in there. That acetate was soft, a finger nail carelessly, or carefully for that matter, drawn across their surface would ruin them. Hinton was sitting at the table, still looking defensively at me.

'What next, Captain?'

Hands down at his side, knuckle towards me. Bugger's got a knife in there, ready to throw. But at whom? Me, or Heidi?

I felt better now I had the recording. 'Next, we revert to the original plan. Only one difference. We go to the broadcasting station a little earlier. Heidi, our beloved cousin, wants to deliver Stocheln's records, and she also wants to have time to show us round before she gets involved with this evening's programme. Don't you, Heidi?'

'I still think you are crazy. You think anybody's going to be deceived by that?'

'Think of the people who live down the road from one of the camps we've named and located so accurately. At first they don't believe us but it might be worth a look. They see lorries and trains? The doubts will grow in the minds of ordinary Germans. That's all we want.'

'I still will not help you voluntarily,' Heidi said.

'Even though you've heard the broadcast ; . .? Even though you've heard the truth . . .?'

'Truth? It doesn't give me any details, I notice, of the number of civilians your bombing has killed, the number of hospitals you've destroyed. It doesn't say anything about the way the Russians fight. A man on my programme last night could tell you things about the Russian Front you wouldn't be able to broadcast, they were so horrible. I'll take you to the studio, and let you make your broadcast, if I have to, to stay alive. But the first chance I get of escaping without you killing me, I'll take it, whether it happens on the doorstep going out of this room, in the street, the studio. You'll need to watch me every second.'

I didn't realize it at the time, but these were just words. She had every intention of seeing that we got safely to the studio, that David Hinton made his broadcast.

'Right,' I said, dropping my knife out of my sleeve, holding it blade forward at waist height close to my body. 'Now's your first chance. Pick up that telephone, ring whoever you normally ring at the broadcasting station when you want a car, and tell them to send one for you. And I'll be listening, to every word.'

CHAPTER FIFTEEN

The car arrived a hundred yards away from the entrance to the Parc des Ouvriers just before quarter to four. François was with them; I didn't trust Hinton. The car stopped, as I'd ordered. I was in the Ministry of Public Works lorry behind, with Heloise's radio plugged to the battery. I sat in the cab wearing the headphones.

The broadcast started at exactly quarter to four. By morse key. It was readable, though faint. The call sign of the station at Haguenau, followed by that of the station in the Parc. It would be inaudible to the operator in Haguenau, who would have become suspicious if he'd heard another station using his code. The call signs were followed by a signals code that meant, *change your call sign to the following before replying*. Normal German Army procedure, to change a call sign if they want to allot it to another station.

The operator in the Parc must have been alerted; he replied immediately, by voice, using the new call sign. Haguenau would hear him coming up, of course, but they would think another station had strayed onto their frequency. They were unlikely to do anything about it immediately for fear of interrupting the passage of an important message.

Then Heloise started again, sending her morse at a volume too low to get to Haguenau, but quite audible a kilometre away in the Parc. The message began with the top priority code. That'd sit the Parc operator to attention. Then came the instruction : *at the conclusion of this message you will acknowledge and then go off the air. Understood.* The Parc operator understood. All normal signals procedure so far.

Then the mesage began; *Your unit with all personnel will move immediately to the following position.* The map reference that followed was on the outskirts of Molsheim, twenty kilometres away. *You will notify us when you are in the new location. Is this message understood? Acknowledge.* The Parc operator acknowledged.

What followed next was a stroke of luck. Heloise, when listening to the new station earlier, had taken note of the message numbers, the ordnance supply numbers, the service stores numbers, and, most importantly, the movement number. Our new message now continued. *This is movement order number GTL/15449/H171 (Becken).*

It was the same movement order number that had brought them to the Parc, with the addition of 1 to the number in the sequence before the name of the authorizing officer. I was taking a chance, but it was worth the risk.

Acknowledge. The Parc operator now acknowledged, reading back the movement order number as is normal in signals procedure. Good. He hadn't queried it. Heloise then sent the last signal.

Radio silence will now be observed until your unit is relocated. The carrier wave switched off. The ether was silent again.

I left the radio in the lorry, walked to the car and exchanged places with François. The driver didn't appear to give a damn who rode in it despite what Heidi had said – so long as Fräulein Lotl was there to vouch for them. The guards on the gate must have felt the same way, and gave only a cursory glance to our identity cards. Hinton was goggle-eyed at the sight of all the soldiers in the Parc. 'How on earth . . .' he started to say, but I cut him off. Several soldiers were strolling beside the path along which we drove; they must have recognized Heidi from her publicity photographs and waved to her. 'We'll be listening,' they said.

We had arrived at the door of the Oestermann House when the Army Unit's klaxon began; all the soldiers in the Parc started to run towards the Headquarters Section. I could have hugged myself; I could have hugged Heloise, too, but perhaps that was something else.

We showed our papers to the guard on the door, then went into the Censor's Office. One man, with a male secretary. At least, I think he was male though I couldn't swear to it. The censor rose to his feet when he saw Heidi. 'That was a wonderful interview last evening,' he said. She bowed modestly, then presented us as her cousins. We showed our passes to him.

He examined them more thoroughly than anyone had before. Heidi explained we were passing through Strasbourg on our way back to Frankfurt, where, as our cards showed, we were employed on chemical research vital to the German war effort, and therefore exempt from military service. 'Chemistry, gentlemen, ah that, alas, is something I know nothing about.'

So much the better for us. Hinton one side of me, Heidi the other. Censor in front. Right hand empty, for handshakes. Left hand bent, ready to catch the knife and jab it forward.

Hinton won't move, I don't think he'll make a move if he knows I'll go for Heidi. Always assuming he's made a pact with her; suspicion grows like a Japanese water-flower once the shell is opened. Did he make love to her? Have they made a deal together? He wouldn't turn me in, on such a slender motive. Maybe he slept with her, and she persuaded him to return to the fold, to the Glory of the Third Reich. That's why I had the recording. In the case I'd put between my feet when I took the Censor's handshake. If he defects, if he starts to make one of his 'Stimme aus Berlin' speeches, I'll throw the prefade switch, cut his microphone, and play the recording. If she tried any tricks – 'the broadcast you are about to hear was made under duress' – I'll throw the switch on her and play the recording.

Heidi explained to the Censor that since we were cousins we were interested in seeing her broadcast: Would that be in order? Yes, it would. He would be honoured to show us round himself. No, that wouldn't be necessary. No trouble, he assured us. We wouldn't dream of it, we assured him. All in all, it was a breathtaking ten minutes before we finally extricated ourselves. 'That was very good,' I said to Heidi. 'Keep it like that and, at ten minutes past seven tonight, you can wave us goodbye and then say what you like.'

'You heard what the soldiers said as we came through the Parc? "We never miss your broadcast." The minute you're out of the studio, I'll broadcast your description to every soldier in that Parc. You'll never get out.'

'That, my dear, is your privilege, and part of our agreement. Once we're through the studio door, you can say what you like.'

'Those soldiers,' Hinton said. 'It won't work . . .'

'Leave the planning to me, Private.'

'Yes, Captain.'

'And now, what's your normal routine, Heidi?' I asked.

'Normally I would go to the control-room and see if they were planning any pre-recordings for me, but Stocheln came out and did those this afternoon. Then I would go to the studio and make pre-recordings. After that, back to my office.'

'No rehearsal for your programme?'

'I don't get the script,' she said, 'until just before the programme.'

'You don't write it?'

She shook her head. 'I'm a broadcaster, not a writer. The scriptwriter brings me a script. I study it for fifteen minutes in the studio, then broadcast it.'

'And that's your idea of truth, eh? The scriptwriter, presumably, is employed by the Gestapo. Or to be more exact, the Ministry of Propaganda. But whatever title you give, it's still the Gestapo. They don't even trust you to see the script until shortly before the broadcast in case you object to the lies it contains. And you defend that system, eh? You're a lackey, my dear, in any country and any language.'

CHAPTER SIXTEEN ·

The last truck left the Parc des Ouvriers at two minutes past five o'clock. Dai Williams watched them go, rubbing his hand, which didn't appear to be broken, but still ached like hell. Several times he'd wondered if he should take the men out of the Parc, through the bushes, via the gap in the wire mesh. But the streets outside were constantly busy and they would have been seen.

A couple of the soldiers in the Parc had wandered down the path to the hut, but by the time they arrived the hut was empty and the sergeant-major's men all hiding in the shrubs. The soldiers had looked in the hut, perhaps hoping to find something to steal, but Jim had locked the padlock, and they'd not dared to force it. One man had looked through the hut's only window. 'Machines in here,' he'd said, and the soldiers went away. For the rest of the day the soldiers seemed content to stroll round the Parc's paths, resting, smoking, chatting. This must be a break between training manoeuvres, Dai Williams reasoned.

And now, they'd all been moved. He'd never doubted Captain Colson would think of something.

Half past five. The door of the Oestermann House opened, and the door guard came out on time. Walked to the guard-house, taking his time. Stood at the guard-house chatting to the gate guard, then went through the wicker gate and presumably home to a hot supper. His was a regular job, eight in the morning until half past five. Routine. Before eight and after half past five the door's not guarded. After all, his function is more to open and close the door than to guard it. The soldiers guard the door to the Parc, the main gate. Not much used; everyone knows the broadcasting station's inside, and that the guards will shoot rather than take a chance.

Six o'clock. Time to go. Gather the lads together, look 'em

over. The chalk and chlorodyne have done the trick and the lads look healthy again, instead of pea-green sick. On Jack's face is a smile that says 'stop smothering us, Sergeant-Major, we're big boys now'. But Dai Williams can't help himself; he cares too much, like a mother who'll overfeed her child all the way to obesity, loving it to death.

The Parc's empty, except for the slow dribble of radio workers going home, the soldering-iron boys, meter readers, office staff who never even bother to listen to a programme.

The Army unit has gone; even swept up its own rubbish and dumped it on the waste pile. Scars on the grass where the field kitchen stood, but they'll grow out in the spring. Along the side of the path by the shrubberies. Down on your belly to cross the open bit, up again, into the shrubberies again, treading your way carefully because you're near the gate. Gate guard, four. Plus a non-com, who stays inside. Telephone to the broadcasting station, so François says. No other communications. Right. Get the lads down. Here they come, the Changing of the Guard. Wouldn't do for the barracks at Wrexham. One Army lorry, four men, plus a non-com. They jump off the lorry, the others clamber on. Bye-bye, bye, see you at eleven.' Bloody disgusting. Where's the discipline? Bloody amateurs. What's happened to the rigidly-disciplined German Army one hears so much about? Wait five minutes. Along comes the Ministry of Public Works lorry, drives up to the gate and stops. 'Stand-by, lads,' Dai whispers. One, two, three, four lads off the back of the lorry, all with papers in their hands, all along the pathway next to the window. Seeing four of them, two of the new guard come to the door. One guard outside the gate to the side of the cab to check the driver's papers. Don't hurt 'em.

'*Hände hoch, bitte.*' The non-com in charge of the guard had gob-stopper eyes that almost dropped out when he saw the Schmeisser the first man in the queue had whipped from under his jacket. Middle of bloody Strasbourg, and they're pulling out Schmeissers! The man checking the lorry driver's papers found himself looking down the barrel of a .45 Colt automatic. Big bullet. It'll blow the back off your head, a right brain-scrambler.

The four men of the guard and the non-com into the back of the lorry. Dai Williams and his lads already in the guard-hut, changing into the uniforms François had thrown from the back of the lorry, each with a name tag on the stringed parcel. Dai Williams smiled. That's what you call planning. Two minutes flat, and the guard had changed for the second time that evening. 'Right-o lads,' he said, 'now let's look like soldiers for a change.' He waved, and the Ministry of Public Works lorry backed, turned into the street, and drove away.

The Censor came walking slowly down the path, full of his own importance. A petty tyrant. If he mattered all that much, he'd have a car. *'Komm, schnell,'* he said to Freddie on the wicker gate. Freddie held out his hand, without speaking.

The Censor put the papers into Freddie's hand; Freddie looked disdainfully at them as if they were Port Said pictures, sneered and handed them back without speaking. The Censor snapped them into his pocket. Then strode through the gate, turned left down the street.

CHAPTER SEVENTEEN

The studio from which Heidi made her broadcast was about twelve feet by eight. It contained a table above which a microphone was suspended, and four chairs. Another microphone was hung in the corner. The walls were entirely covered in cloth-bag sound-proofing.

A 'cubicle' was attached to the studio. It had been marked as such on the plan the brigadier had shown me of a typical German broadcasting set-up. All the items I'd been told to look for were here. There was a control-panel in front of the large glass window at which the control engineer, the producer, and his secretary sat; the bank of record-playing turntables along the other three sides of the room, broken only by the door into the corridor, and the door into the studio itself. The prefade switch was on the panel and marked. The lights were low in the studio and cubicle; spot lights focused on the table from which Heidi would make her broadcast. A loudspeaker hung from the wall above the panel, and two telephones were on a shelf within easy reach of the control engineer's hand. The brigadier had briefed me about them; one was an internal telephone which connected to the major control-room; the other an outside line. The programme was not censored in the studio, since its contents had been recorded or written in advance and approved; all Heidi had to do was stitch the separate portions together, linking them with her pre-written narrations.

Technically, the producer's job was a sinecure, though you wouldn't have thought so to see the self-important way he sat at the control-panel, a pencil held in his hand as if it were a baton, a duelling scar like a badge of rank running down his cheek. He deigned to notice me, offered me a seat with a gesture that said, 'don't disturb, genius at work'.

I said I'd prefer to stand at the back. He couldn't have cared less where I was. Heidi ran through her introductions. The secretary timed them, the producer marked his script. Now was the dangerous time; Hinton and Heidi were in the studio together, and I couldn't hear what they were saying, what they might be planning. Heidi had given the Stocheln records to the engineer, who'd placed them on a side-table. During a break in the rehearsal, he took the records out of their cases and looked at them.

The producer's secretary gave me a copy of the script and the lay-out, as she called it, a running order of each of the items.

19.00-19.01 Opening music.

19.01-19.01.15 Opening announcement, live, studio LOTL.

19.01.15-19.01.45 *Deutsche-Gramophon 661223 Ersehnte Freiheit.*

(Stirring battle march.)

19.01.45-19.02.00 INTRODUCTION : LOTL.

19.02.00-19.12.00 INTERVIEW : LOTL SG113/1-4.

The time was approaching 19.00 hours. They were still

arguing over the programme timing. The record engineer said, 'God, it's hot in here,' and took off his jacket. The producer, dressed in double-breasted, navy-blue suit, shiny at the elbows, a white shirt, grubby round the neck, and a dark brown tie, shot a baleful look at the man in his shirt and braces. 'After the war,' he muttered, 'perhaps we will get some respectable staff again.' The engineer made an international sign behind the producer's back.

Heidi was looking at me. Three minutes to go. Would she, wouldn't she? Would Hinton, wouldn't Hinton? I didn't give a damn now I had the recording.

'I wonder if it would be possible for me to hear the start of this recording?' I whispered to the record engineer, taking Hinton's talk from my suitcase.

The producer thundered. 'Shut up, please! Absolute silence. How can I concentrate with all this chattering?' You'd have been forgiven for thinking he was producing *The Ring*. The record engineer grimaced at his back, cleared an acetate disc from a turntable, and deftly flicked side one of Hinton's talk into its place. He used a spare pair of headphones to locate the start of the talk, then handed them to me so that I could listen. It was a good recording, clean and crisp. I lifted the needle, and set it back so that it hovered over the start of the talk.

Heidi was talking to David Hinton. He looked at me. What were they saying? It couldn't be anything important; they had no way of knowing we weren't listening. Or had they? On the loudspeaker was a regimental march, from a live broadcast in Strasbourg Town Hall, or so the announcer had said when he introduced the item. No news bulletin tonight. That's odd. I'd heard the news bulletin when I'd listened to the programme.

'No news bulletin?' I asked the secretary. She shook her head.

'After the programme, from now on,' she said. The producer shot us a disapproving look; it was the only one of which his scar-slashed face seemed capable. Two minutes before seven o'clock.

Mental check. Me here, with Hinton's speech recorded.

Hinton there, with his speech memorized and in a script in his pocket.

Dai Williams in the guard-house at the gate, to keep people out of the Parc, to cover our dash when this lot was over.

The soldiers gone from the Parc.

The road mines planted, and François's men standing by.

An aeroplane on its way.

And, last of all, Heidi. Will she; won't she? It no longer matters. If she doesn't cooperate, if she doesn't introduce Davin Hinton as arranged, we cut her off here at the panel, and we play the Hinton recording.

The control engineer went into the studio, checked the microphone on its stand, the cue light. Kicked the spare microphone plug to make sure it was in properly, then stood talking to Heidi. What about? Their obvious, mutual hatred of the producer? The control engineer came out again, went to the bank of acetates, selected one, set it on the table so that the needle was hovering over the first groove, and sat down.

'What was that all about?' the producer asked, but the control engineer didn't answer him.

'Ready to go on the air. Stand by studio.' He was in charge of the programme and started to run it like an automaton. The control-room telephone buzzed; the control engineer didn't pick it up but pressed a button inside it, to assure them he was ready and alert; the second-hand climbed the face of the clock. It was hot in the cubicle. The brass band ended twenty seconds after one minute before seven o'clock. Forty seconds to go. Silence on the air for eight seconds. Hot as hell. The station announcement, spoken somewhere else and fed into our loudspeaker. '*Hier ist der Deutsche Rundfunk aus Strasbourg.*' Silence again. I reached into my pocket and pulled out the Colt, hiding it in the sweating palm of my hand. I clicked back the barrel as noiselessly as I could, but the producer's secretary turned and looked at me, pleading for silence. I was standing in a pool of darkness, and she could not see the gun in my hand. Ten seconds to go.

Claustrophobic. Station signal, a drum-beat switched on and off abruptly.

'Stand by,' the control engineer said. I'd said the same thing many times in the same atmosphere. Stand by, ready to jump. I almost checked to see if my parachute strap was fastened. Five, four, three, two, one seconds. The red light came on. The control engineer said, 'Now.' The record engineer lowered the needle onto the first groove of the opening music, and whipped the potentiometer open. 'You've got it,' he said. As yet I could hear nothing. Then the control engineer opened one of the many potentiometers on his desk, and the opening music swelled out of the loudspeaker, pompous but suitably majestic. The control engineer allowed the music to grow, adjusting its volume constantly, then, on a certain bar, he flipped open another potentiometer, pressed a switch. A light came on in front of Heidi; she leaned into the microphone and, against the background of those solemn chords, said, '*TAGESSCHAU*.'

I could see her mouth work, but I couldn't hear the words. Nor could the producer. He was startled, jerked into life. 'Sorry,' the control engineer said, and flipped up the prefade switch.

'It went out?' the producer demanded.

'Yes, it went out. I wasn't on studio prefade so we couldn't hear it, that's all.'

'But it WAS broadcast?'

'Yes, sir, I assure you, it *was* broadcast.'

Dai Williams handed two canisters to Freddie, two to Frank. 'You left,' he said to Freddie. 'You right,' to Frank. 'You've got five minutes.' Freddie and Frank started marching briskly down the paths of the Parc des Ouvriers.

By seven o'clock, the Censor was already at home in his apartment on the Avenue de la Paix. His wife had prepared a supper of kalbshaxe with chick-peas. '*Schön,*' he said, sniffing its odour from the plate. He heard the music start, heard it fade down slightly, and his mouth uttered the word, '*Tagesschau*'. He raised his hand solemnly. 'Absolute silence now,' he said. His wife had gone back into the kitchen and there was no one to hear him. He cut off a small piece of the kalbshaxe and put it in his mouth.

Seven o'clock and thirty seconds. Henk pressed the switch in the back of the telephone operators' desk in the telephone exchange. Nothing apparently happened. The many conversations continued on already connected lines. But the continuous trippings of relays stopped. No one was bothered. Sometimes, they went as long as a minute without receiving an incoming call. The SS man was monitoring a call from a house off the Place d'Austerlitz to the office of the Controller of the Bassin Vauban. The caller appeared to be saying he couldn't get in for work that evening, but he was taking a long time saying it. The call was being wire-recorded.

One minute past seven o'clock. The lorry from the Ministère des Travaux Publiques was parked at the end of the Avenue Grenouille, by the wine market. Big decision. Should the lorry be inside the area of the Parc des Ouvriers, or outside it? Outside. Then, if it's needed . . . Three men walking along the Avenue, and a woman. François stepped out. Flashed his identity badge, an impressive-looking card with *Ministère des Travaux Publiques* printed across the top in bold capitals.

'I wouldn't go up the avenue,' he said.
'*Pourquoi pas, eh?*'
'There's a gas leak. Could be an explosion.'
'*Merde.*' They turned and went into the cross-street. They knew about gas leaks, and the *Maquis*. Ask no questions, salute the brave ones, and *futez le camp* . . .

19.01.15 : The music began, *Ersehnte Freiheit*. The sort of music that automatically brings you to attention. Thirty seconds of it. Fade down. Cue Heidi. Here comes her announcement. I stepped out of the darkness into a cone of light from the spot lamp over the control desk. 'I've got a gun here, so you will please do as I tell you. I am a British Army Officer, and if any one of you disobeys me, I will shoot

129

him. Or her,' I said, catching an involuntary movement from the secretary.

Heidi had begun to speak. 'And now, dear listeners, I have a surprise for you; but first of all, a mystery. Who can remember this voice . . . ?'

At this departure from the officially approved text, the producer started forward. I put the Colt behind his ear. 'The Gestapo will kill me,' he said. It wasn't a very original thought. 'Gestapo or me, which do you prefer?'

He sank back in his seat.

David Hinton was speaking. Using the brigadier's script. The 'mystery voice' idea belonged to the brigadier, too, taken from ITMA, a BBC broadcast of the time.

'I have lived for many years in Germany,' Davin Hinton said, 'and have had many opportunities to study the workings of the German High Command. Which is rather surprising, as I am an Englander.'

The Censor had his telephone in his hand and kalbshaxe all over the table cloth where it had slopped from the plate, and spluttered from his mouth. He could hear the brr-brrr of the ringing tone. There was no answer. 'Come on,' he said, listening to the voice coming from his radio, trying to memorize its words for future reference.

The Gestapo Officer in charge of Radio Censorship was sitting in his office. From his desk, a loudspeaker was broadcasting the programme '*Tagesschau*'. He was holding a telephone to his ear. He could hear the sound of the ringing of the instrument at the other end, or so he thought.

'*Um Gottes Will*, answer the telephone !' he screamed into the instrument.

The telephone exchange staff sat back relaxed. 'Quiet night tonight,' Anne remarked, slipping off her headset for a moment. 'Do you realize we haven't had a single incoming call for over a minute?'

The SS man was still listening to the conversation between the Place d'Austerlitz and the Bassin Vauban. The wire-recorder whirred. The man in the Place d'Austerlitz was describing his symptoms in detail. The face of the SS man was tinged with green. He was squeamish of medical matters.

An Army motor-cycle combination carrying three soldiers was half-way down the Avenue Grenouille. They had stopped. By the manhole cover. The soldiers sat still, looking round the deserted street.

'Stay there,' François muttered, 'just stay, right there, for another minute, you bastards.'

Davin Hinton was sticking word for word to the brigadier's script. Heidi had identified him as the '*Stimme aus Berlin*', and had promised the listeners he would tell them his story in his own way, without interruption from her.

The producer had had some kind of heart attack, of that I was certain. He'd slumped in his seat, his face mottled and red. The secretary unfastened his tie, but then I waved her back into her seat. I was pointing the gun in the general direction of Heidi, behind the glass. David Hinton was looking at her, broadcasting his story to her. It was a first-class performance.

His script was open in front of him, but I could tell he wasn't using it. The control engineer sat very still, his hands on the control-desk. My recording of Hinton's speech was on the turntable, with the needle down, following Hinton's live broadcast. If he departed from his script at any time, I'd order the control engineer to cut the studio and play the recording. The record engineer was wearing his headphones, listening to the recording, eyes flicked here and there; watch them all, watch them all. The secretary sat like stone, the producer like a side of butchered beef. I could tell the control engineer was alert, ready for the first slip. I put the gun behind his ear. 'Take it easy,' I said. 'You don't want to be a hero, do you?'

He didn't reply.

The officer in charge of Radio Censorship slammed down the telephone, after the fourth number he had dialled did not answer. He flung open his window. 'Get me a truck with twenty men and a car. Fast as possible,' he shouted. Then he started to run down the two flights of stairs to the ground floor.

A staff-colonel was screaming into a telephone in a lavish office in Berlin. 'What do you mean, they don't answer?' The impersonal voice of the military switchboard operator came back to him in slow, measured tones. 'I'm ringing Strasbourg Central,' he said, 'but they do not answer. Perhaps they are busy . . .'

The staff-colonel suddenly felt a tightening in his chest. Oh, my God, don't say his heart was going to start fluttering again. He sat back in his chair, took control of himself. 'Right,' he said, speaking carefully and slowly, avoiding excitement. 'Please get me a priority call to the Luftwaffe station at Obersteigen. I want to speak immediately to the highest-ranking officer there.'

A bang in the Rue des Ouvriers, and a hole appeared in the road following the line of the culvert carrying the electricity cables. All the power went out in that street, and a hole in the road stretched from wall to wall, even across the pavement. The hole was six feet deep in places. Rue Clemenceau, same story. Rue de la Paix, Rue Bordeaux, all had gaping craters impassable by vehicles.

Bang in the Boulevard Chevreuil. Misnamed a boulevard, it was no wider than a street, and the factory which collapsed halfway along blocked it with rubble over ten feet high. Avenue d'Anvers, same story, Rue du Petit Rhin, ditto.

The mine didn't explode in the Rue de Séverin. '*Merde,*' François said, after waiting thirty seconds. He ran down the street, along which screaming people were already starting to run. Desmond and Arneuil ran shouting with him. 'Get away, the street's going up too.'

The pall of dust that had risen from the other avenues and streets had begun to settle above the Séverin and bricks and timber were floating through it; one old lady had dropped to the ground and Arneuil took her by the ankles, flipped her onto her back, and pushed her like a wheel barrow behind a low wall.

François had reached the manhole cover. An unexploded bomb's a fearful thing; the slightest jar can set it off. He put the irons he carried into the manhole cover, twisted them and lifted. The cover came up. *Merde*. The fuse had pulled out of the detonator coupling. *Merde!* He took a short length of fuse from his pocket to replace the burned one, slipped it into the detonator tube, and, crouching down with his head in the hole, he lit it. Two seconds to put the manhole cover back in position, then turn and run like hell. Desmond and Arneuil followed him, running like hell too, but they were still within the bomb blast when the street exploded, picked them up and threw them like rolling dice along the pavement. Arneuil felt his arm snap, Desmond landed with his head scraping the wall, and François hit a doorway with his thigh, hearing the sickening snap of a bone.

Seven minutes after seven o'clock. David Hinton was halfway through his broadcast. A lorry load of men was on its way from the Gestapo barracks followed by a Mercedes-Benz in which sat the officer in charge of Radio Censorship; the lorry and the car were both doing sixty miles an hour, their engines racing, angry spumes of smoke vibrating from their exhausts; both had klaxons screaming, a harsh, high-pitched, alternating note that drove fear into the hearts of those who heard it.

Except two of François's men, in the doorway of the horse-meat butcher's shop. They were looking at their watches.

The lorry was in front of the disused warehouse when the first explosion came. It blew the front out of the warehouse and stopped the lorry dead. The Mercedes-Benz ran into the back of the lorry. Then the building slid out on itself, rubble rolling and roaring into the street, filling it from side to side with baulks of timber, masonry debris, bricks, tiles, broken, flying glass, twisted steel that completely covered the lorry and the car locked into its back. The plume of dust and of smoke rose high above the houses on each side of the street. There was no flame, no further explosions, but the street was impassably blocked.

I looked round the cubicle. I was sure the producer had died. It did not matter, I'd seen too much of death already to care about one over-fat, self-indulgent man. The control engineer was sitting still, his fingers spread before him on the surface of his control-desk. The secretary beside the producer quietly wept. The record engineer was bending over the turntable, playing the record of David Hinton. But both Heidi and I were listening to David Hinton's voice on the loudspeaker performing the brigadier's text. This David Hinton was different from anything I had ever seen; it was as if, finally, he'd found himself. He was quietly confident, masterful in his technique. This, I felt, was what he had been destined to do, to sit alone in the silence of a broadcasting station and send his calm, measured, cultured voice out to millions of people. I could understand why he had held so much power as the *'Stimme aus Berlin'*. His voice, his manner, were hypnotically compulsive, entirely credible. One could not imagine lies or calumny coming from such a mouth, one could not imagine such a person lending himself to anything false.

'It doesn't matter to me,' David Hinton said, 'that I've risked my life to come here to make this broadcast to you this evening. All I ask is that those of you who've listened to me for the past ten minutes, will reflect on what I have said. And then will refuse to be part of the greatest collective act of barbarity the civilized world has ever known.

'Germany and Great Britain can be united again, can work together for the benefit of a mighty Europe; but only if those who direct your feet along the present path of infamy can be overthrown and destroyed. You will be conquered by the Allied Armies; don't force us to destroy the entire manhood of the German nation at the same time.'

The German soldiers had abandoned the lorries and cars and were pouring over the road blocks, through holes in the road the charges had made. The whole area surrounding the Parc des Ouvriers had been blacked-out when the explosive charges which ripped the road surfaces tore the cables. In each street rubble and smoke from the demolition fought with the flames from burst gas-mains, plumes of fire as much as three metres high. Water poured out of burst water mains, flooding along the street to add to the confusion; the soldiers fought their way through the holocaust as if at the heart of a flaming battle.

The Oestermann House gleamed like a fairy castle on the black lake of the Parc. Dai Williams and Jim had gone from room to room along the ground floor, opening windows and pulling curtains to let out the light. The Oestermann House had its own supply which sprang to life when the power was cut. Its diesel engines thudded in the night, competing with the roar and crackle and rumble of the demolition all round the Parc.

Freddie and Frank placed the canisters, and lit them; two red and two green, marking the ends of the lawn. The bright jewel of the Oestermann House lay at one end of the lawn, a perfect landing mark for the plane which came in low from the east. In the sky, ten thousand feet above the light plane, were Lancaster Bombers on their way to Frankfurt. The searchlight beams from the Siegfried Line were directed at them; the timed fuses of the anti-aircraft shells set to explode among them. The German radar was plotting them; no one, it seemed, was paying any attention to the smaller plane that skimmed across the sky towards the red and green flares of the Parc des Ouvriers, the lights of the Oestermann House, and set its wheels neatly on the end of the lawn, where, earlier that day, the bivouacs of the German Army had been pitched.

David Hinton finished his broadcast.

The main power lead came in through the floor, around, and up to the control-desk. I put two shots from the Colt through it. The studio immediately was dead. The emergency lights came on. The telephone from the control-room rang. I told the engineer and the secretary to go into the studio and lie flat on their faces; I left the producer where he was. Flick of the gun towards Heidi but the gesture embraced Davin Hinton. 'Well done, lad,' I said, 'now out of here, rapid, both of you.'

They went ahead of me. I jammed the arm of a lamp through the two handles of the double studio door, making it impossible to open from inside, and went into the corridor. Short. Leads to a lobby. Second floor. 'Down the stairs.' The lift is coming up. That'd be someone from the control-room wondering what the hell had happened in the studio.

By now the duty-announcer in the continuity suite somewhere else in the building would be playing music and apologizing for the programme break, promising them he'd have *'Tagesschau'* back on the air as soon as possible. He'd have heard the Hinton broadcast, of course, but there was no reason he should stop it. No one in the station had that sort of responsibility without a direct telephone call from one of the station bosses or from the Gestapo, and we'd fixed that in the telephone exchange.

Two floors down. No one in the front lobby. Across it, and then out of the front door. Good man. Dai's there, waiting for us. Surprised when he sees Heidi; beckons at her with his gun.

'Where are you taking me?' Heidi said, stopping running.

'Nowhere. Just getting you out of there. Away from that continuity suite and microphone.'

I could see the plane taxiing rapidly across the lawn towards us, about fifty yards away. When it reached the flare line, John and Jack ran in, and turned it around, and I beckoned to Hinton.

'Come on,' I said, 'let's get out of here.'

But he stood there. Immobile. I stopped. Heidi was holding his hand. 'I'm not coming back,' he said.

I beckoned to him with the gun. 'Come on, cut the crap, and get aboard that plane.'

He shook his head. 'I'm not coming back with you,' he said.

I knew he meant it. 'They'll tear you alive after that broadcast,' I said. 'But presumably you know that . . .?

Heidi was smiling at me, turned to Hinton and smiled some more. When the long fuse of cruelty, deceit, and revenge is set alight is it always the thoughtlessness of a man which has fired it . . .? The bitch. She was taking her revenge on me, all right. I'd beaten her over the broadcast, she'd beaten me over Hinton. The next day she'd have Hinton back at the microphone, reading another script, but this one a full recantation, written by the Gestapo.

No time left. I could hear the chatter of Schmeissers in the streets along the Parc, hear the boom of the hand grenades that François's men were dropping from the roof-tops to delay the Germans. They wouldn't be able to hold them for many more minutes, but that was all the time we needed. If we got a move on.

'I'm not coming,' Hinton said.

'He's not coming,' Heidi said.

I looked at both of them, standing together. She'd won, of course. I'd made the broadcast and lost the broadcaster. 'Go on, Captain,' he said, 'get in your plane and go back to England.' Just something about the way he said the words 'Captain' and 'England'. On his twisted lips they were terms of derision. I didn't give a damn about England. But I couldn't stand the way he said 'Captain'. The Colt jumped in my hand, and the shot got him square in his chest and bowled him over backwards, breaking the grip of their hands.

The bitch never even looked down at him. She knew I wouldn't shoot her. We turned and ran, looking backwards over our shoulders. She never once looked down at him lying on the ground. She was watching us run, standing there quite still, a light wind plucking the hem of that woollen dress.

They'd turned the plane and we climbed aboard. Dai first, Freddie and Frank, John and Jack, Jim, and me last.

I tapped the pilot on his shoulder and waved my arm. The engine of the plane screamed to high revs, and he took it all the way to full before he jerked off the wheel brakes and let it go into the wind, running along the lawn like a bullet. Plenty of room for take off. Course north-west, for England.

I didn't look down.

EPILOGUE

And that was the end of Operation Rundfunk, or so I thought.

On the plane we had nothing to do but dodge through the flak and relax. I chatted with the lads. I'd seen little of them, knew nothing about them. Jobs are often done that way, one group here, one group there, and rarely the 'twain shall meet'. Once we blew a bridge from both ends and north never met south.

'Come on, lads,' I said, 'no names, no pack drill, but who killed Tony?'

I looked round the cabin of the plane, studied each face in turn. Not one of them was guilty. I'd stake my third pip on that. I looked at Dai. 'All right Dai,' I said. 'You tell me?'

'Only a guess, mind. . .'

'I'll settle for a guess. . .'

'Tony was very close to the brigadier, sir. Early on we all thought he was a bit odd, if you get my meaning. . .'

'Tony or the brigadier . . .?'

'Tony. Seemed like he was all right and all wrong, almost as if, well, you know how you can smell a copper . . .?'

It figured. The brigadier was just the man to have a plant. Watching me? Or watching Hinton? The latter, most likely. I couldn't see the brigadier trusting anybody, especially not Hinton, after the '*Stimme aus Berlin*' broadcasts. So the wily old fox had planted a copper in the squad, and somehow Hinton had found out. Hinton had killed Tony.

It made sense.

I reported to the brigadier after my arrival in England. He told me to sit down and played me a wire recording of the last broadcast Hinton had made. I tried not to look smug when Hinton's voice came on, clear and strong, exactly the way I'd remembered him. He said he'd been back to

England – 'to see for himself' – and had returned to the Fatherland more convinced than ever of the decadence of the British and the superiority of the *Herrenvolk*.

That was not in the script.

I looked at the brigadier. 'You bloody fool,' he said, 'you absolute, utter, bloody fool.'

The broadcast continued in the best *'Stimme aus Berlin'* style and the brigadier made me listen to the bitter end.

How the hell had they done it? Dead simple, really. It didn't take the brigadier long to work out that Hinton and Heidi had pre-recorded the talk while I'd been out that morning. They'd telephoned to Stocheln to come and cut the acetate disc. But when had the Stocheln recording been switched in the cubicle? Suddenly I remembered that control engineer going into the studio, kicking the plugs to make certain they were securely home. Heidi must have been talking at that moment, saying something like – 'Don't ask any questions; play the Stocheln recording; keep the cubicle on local prefade so that man can only hear what we say on the microphone, not what is actually being transmitted.'

The Gestapo were trying to get to the broadcasting station not to stop the broadcast, but to welcome back an old friend.

'You absolute, utter, bloody fool,' the brigadier said. Then I had to explain why I'd shot his old Etonian buddy.

Sometimes, in the evening, I tune my radio and listen to *'Tagesschau'* with Heidi Lotl. I like to think that perhaps she knows I'm listening. But I suppose she's forgotten all about me and David Hinton.

Colin Forbes

TARGET FIVE 40p

'Danger and excitement more hair-raising than I remember in years' – DAILY MIRROR

'In the Maclean mould' – EVENING STANDARD

No quarter is asked or given when a top Russian oceanographer defects across the Arctic icefields with plans of their submarine network. The Americans send in dog teams and an unconventional trio under Anglo-Canadian agent Keith Beaumont. The Russians use everything they have in an increasingly bloody life-or-death struggle to win him back . . .

'Frightening as a nuclear bomb' – IRISH TIMES

'Simply super in chills and thrills'
    – AMERICAN PUBLISHERS WEEKLY

'Keeps the reader on the edge of his chair'
    – DAILY TELEGRAPH

'Utterly realistic and gripping action'
    – SPECTATOR

Leslie Thomas

George Bruce

THE WARSAW UPRISING   60p
Illustrated

'Horses had long since been eaten . . . now it
was the turn of the dogs'.

On 1 August 1944, the people of Warsaw
rose against their Nazi oppressors. With an
almost unbelievable courage, the ill-equipped
Polish Secret Army held out for sixty-three
days and nights under a relentless barrage
from German artillery, planes and tanks.

Did the Russian army deliberately stand by
while the Poles were crushed?

Did the Americans and the British do all in
their power to help Warsaw?

These and many other challenging questions
are answered in an enthralling, objective
history.

'One of the most heroic, as well as tragic,
episodes of the Second World War . . . mov-
ingly related in a valuable book'

      — ARMY QUARTERLY

Walter Langer

THE MIND OF ADOLF HITLER   50p

'One of the most remarkable documents of
the Second World War'
        — TIMES EDUCATIONAL SUPPLEMENT

This top-secret study, written in 1943 for the
Office of Strategic Services, is a startlingly
accurate predictive analysis of the Hitler per-
sonality and a fascinating attempt to apply
psychoanalytic insight to warfare.

Dr Langer's analysis probes Hitler's dual per-
sonality, his hatred of the Jews, his sexual
pathologies and perversions, his troubled
childhood, his manias, phobias, and contradic-
tions.

'A *tour de force* of science blended with
imagination' — SUNDAY TELEGRAPH